Iceland

Iceland

JIM KRUSOE

Dalkey Archive Press

Library of Congress Cataloging-in-Publication Data:

Krusoe, James, 1942-
        Iceland / Jim Krusoe.— 1st ed.
            p. cm.
        ISBN 1-56478-314-6 (acid-free paper)
            1. Eccentrics and eccentricities—Fiction. I. Title.
    PS3561.R873 I28 2002
    813'.54—dc21

                                                    2002019295

Partially funded by a grant from the Illinois Arts Council, a state agency.

Dalkey Archive Press books are published by the Center for Book Culture, a
nonprofit organization with offices in Chicago and Normal, Illinois.

www.centerforbookculture.org

Printed on permanent/durable acid-free paper and bound in the United
States of America.

"I've learnt to ride, at least to ride a pony
        Taken a lot of healthy exercise,
On barren mountains and in valleys stony . . ."
                        — W. H. Auden, *Letters from Iceland*

"How strange it is to be gone in a minute!   A man
Signs a shovel and so he digs . . ."
                        — Ted Berrigan, *Sonnet LXXXVIII*

For Jenny

I

I had been dying little by little and bit by bit, I thought. On some days I felt fine, as if the animal, or machine, or whatever I was at that moment, could easily believe that the whole thing, this dying business, had been only a bad dream, although a waking one to be sure, which had somehow leaked into my mind while I was waiting at a street corner for a traffic light as all around me cars went about their business, their exhaust spewing into my lungs, their radios hurting my ears. But the catch was that they would continue on doing this forever, and I would not.

My name, by the way, is Paul.

But then the light would change and I would be somewhere else, in a pet store, or sitting on a stool in a piano bar, and I'd been wrong; I was fine until the next time I blinked again, when there it would be, back and grinning. So I had been suffering for a long time, in one way or another, and at last it seemed as if the end was growing near: I had finally given up resistance to the idea of going through life carrying someone else's organ inside of me — and either the procedure would work or it wouldn't.

So it was on Dr. Pearlman's advice I finally boarded the big, blue bus that passed by the Institute, where I was supposed to, as he put it, "look the organs over," and to find one that I liked. Then came the first surprise. No sooner had I stepped off the bus straight onto a rolled-up newspaper than I twisted my ankle, and when I looked up I saw that the place looked nothing like I'd imagined. I checked the address. When Dr. Pearlman had mentioned that the Institute was housed in a former villa, I'd pictured something out of Pompeii, light and airy, and full of vines, with maybe even a baby volcano looming in the background. But there it was, right in the middle of town, built on classic lines but of dull, gray granite, dark and solid, next to an ice-making plant and surrounded not by vines, but heavy, leafless trees, their arms stretched hopelessly toward the sun. Worse, its narrow windows looked as if they'd been stabbed into the walls by a knife, or possibly an axe, and its corners were anchored by four huge stones, like four heavy cenotaphs yet to be inscribed. The overall effect, it seemed to me at that moment, was that the whole building was slowly sinking into the ground.

I limped up the stairs to the huge, bronze doors, and looked for a buzzer. Where there should have been one, there was only a small brass plate, about the size of a business card, with the name of the Institute in capital letters. I knocked, but against the heavy doors was unable to produce a sound. I tried again, with both hands, and again nothing came back. So I pushed lightly against one of them, and lo, it swung open, but the next surprise was that once I was inside there was no reception area, no waiting room with magazines, and no nurse dressed in a starched white uniform asking me to fill out my insurance forms, which I was pleased to have brought, just in case.

Nor were there men in white smocks, nor wall-high stainless steel freezers, nor anything else I had imagined. Instead there was only a bright hallway, done in the pink marble I'd expected to find outside, running from right to left, lined with statues of nymphs and scandalous satyrs, crumbling griffins and shameless naiads. I could find no instructions anywhere, but directly in front of me, on the facing wall, was one more set of doors, this time made of carved wood. I knocked and waited, knocked and waited. Finally I leaned my shoulder into one half (there weren't any handles) and it opened with a screech onto a large swimming pool, filled, judging by the smell, with saltwater.

I stepped inside and inhaled. In addition to the salt, I could also catch the semen-y odor of chlorine. It turned out I was standing next to a red bucket of bleach. Then I blinked, because I had not been prepared in the least for what I saw next. There, twenty feet away, within the blue-tiled borders of the pool, were the very organs I'd come to visit: the bloated, spongy butterflies of lungs, the shy parentheses of kidneys, the lurid exclamation marks of livers, the cheerful blimps of stomachs, the loopy daydreams of intestines, the schools of tiny pancreas, and dark, brooding spleens, all drifting across the pool's still surface like floaters along the back of an eyeball, all sleeping in their Olympic-sized waterbed, dreaming. There was no roof, but above them, about twenty feet off the surface of the water, was a steamy sheet of plastic tarp, hung (it looked like) to keep the heat in, and maybe also to catch any stray impurities.

3

I stood there watching, and already I could feel the artificial fibers of my shirt gluing themselves to my back in the humid, warm air. But strangely — as opposed to my earlier, more futuristic expectations about the place — and as unlikely as it seemed, the organs spread out there before me apparently were thriving.

At that very moment my eye caught a movement at the far end of the pool: the most beautiful woman I had ever seen was emerging from the liquid. I stood breathless as her small fingers clasped the two silvery sweating handrails, and her shoulders bent slightly from the weight of her scuba gear. Her full lips, I could see, were ever-so-slightly bruised by the mouthpiece of her breathing apparatus, and the shape of her full breasts was accentuated by the dark, nylon straps across her chest. Panting slightly, she pulled herself onto the tiled deck, and stood dripping, one small foot naked, and the other temporarily concealed by a single black swim fin.

Then she turned, and even from that distance I could see that she was blushing. I remained quiet, uncertain whether I should approach or not, but she waved me closer. "I'm sorry," she said, "I don't get very many guests, and I didn't expect to see anyone today."

She pointed to a thick, pink towel draped over a statue of a mermaid and made a motion, so I half-tossed it over to her. She loosened her hair, rich and luxurious, and rubbed it with the towel as if she were completely alone, and suddenly I was the one who felt embarrassed. Maybe I'd got the date wrong, or even the place. I checked my pocket for the card Dr. Pearlman had given me, but I was correct.

"Excuse me," I said. "I hadn't expected to see anyone here

either, and certainly not anyone like you. I guess I imagined this place would mostly be made up of vats and tubes and things. Dr. Pearlman," I said, but the woman seemed not to recognize his name, "suggested it might be a good idea for me to come down to see the organs, and maybe even pick myself out a good one. My name is Paul."

"Oh," she said, and blushed again. "I'm terrible at keeping appointments. My name is Emily."

I waited as Emily unhooked herself from the heavy scuba gear and removed the swim fin (both her feet were slender, with delicate pink veins along their tops, but the one that had been wearing the fin was slightly chaffed). Then she took the tanks and dragged them out of the way, the resulting sound a peculiar, half bell-like, half-heavy scrape. For a brief second I thought maybe I should offer to give her a hand, but realized that she might well be insulted; after all this was part of a medical procedure.

"Well," Emily picked up the conversation where it had left off, "in a way you were right." She told me that the place started out pretty much the way I'd imagined it, with vats and tubes and fancy instruments for monitoring the state of everything, but then the doctors running the business discovered that the organs weren't lasting as long as they'd hoped, that somehow the transition from the sterile vats to a real live body wasn't working very well. Also, even if the organs did last, they just weren't performing up to the doctors' high standards. Finally, after a lot of scientific experiments about antibody resistance and environmental flexibility, the doctors found the answer was something comparatively simple. There was a complicated name for it, of course, but really it just turned out that those organs only really needed to keep in contact with the human body. "All those earlier organs had been lonely," Emily said, "and in between leaving their old bodies and finding a new one, they'd started to pine away, like people in a refugee camp."

Then Emily stopped for a minute, as if she noticed something, and walked over to a wall where a long-handled net with special foam padding was hanging. Putting a finger over her lips to indicate I shouldn't make a sound, she took the net and slowly maneuvered it out toward the center of the pool. Suddenly I noticed that one of the spleens in the middle seemed to be in trouble, and was sort of vibrating. She lowered her net to neatly scoop it out of the water, then in the same graceful motion swung it around to hover above a blue plastic trash bucket. "Would you mind taking off the lid?" she asked. "I'm afraid this little fellow isn't going to make it."

I opened the trash and Emily flipped it in. She hung the dripping net back on the wall.

"In any case," Emily continued, "those first scientists decided that instead of having their organs cared for by machines, it might be better to hire a real person to come by several times a week to vacuum up whatever debris may have fallen into the pool, but mostly to swim around with the little guys (that's what I call them)." She shrugged. "It's my job to skim off sloughed cells, and pull out dead organs, but most important, I brush up against the live ones as I swim, and sometimes I hum to them through the mouthpiece of my breathing apparatus. What I'm trying to say here is that I stimulate them however I can — I was a pre-veterinary major and was on the swim team before I dropped out of college. In any case, ever since I started working here, the patients' survival rate has gone way up." Suddenly she seemed self-conscious.

"Can you help me with these weights around my waist?" Emily asked. "I'm afraid the clasp is kind of slippery."

And I have to say it was, the clasp was very slippery with whatever substance they used to keep the organs alive — and in the process I found my fingers dangerously close to Emily's skin. Then all at once several of them were actually sliding against it, and then — and you'll have to believe me here — almost against my will, my entire arsenal of fingers was running rapidly up and down Emily's sleek skin on their own, just as the bottom of Emily's two-piece bathing suit (light blue, a floral pattern) fell to the ground with a thwack.

"Oh my God," she gasped, and then all at once she was loosening my tie (honestly, I don't know why I was wearing a tie that day — I guess it seemed professional) and helping me off with my madras jacket, my shirt, trousers, shoes, underwear, and socks. Then the weights fell to the floor, narrowly missing my injured ankle, and then — exactly how, I can't say — the top of her swimsuit somehow got unhooked, and I found the two of us falling together onto a spare roll of plastic tarp.

Then amazingly — what a day this was turning out to be! — the two of us, having begun somewhat precariously atop the tarp, moved to the tiled floor, and then over to the throbbing pool pump, where we continued with this — believe me — completely atypical, even frantic behavior until, still clinging helplessly to each other, as in a trance, we staggered to the kiddy pool at the far end where the smaller organs — corneas, testicles, ovaries, and such — were kept, and there, in this highly unusual setting, made love again, but this time a lot more carefully.

Stunned, we both sat and, avoiding the glances of the corneas, stared at the ground for a while (who knows how long?), until finally, holding hands in an embarrassed silence, we returned to where we'd left our clothes in two damp heaps, one small and one large, and we dressed.

"Emily," I began, "I don't know what came over me. Once I read an article in Dr. Pearlman's office how when people are placed in a life and death situation sometimes time speeds up, or slows down, I forget which, and they fall in love, and then make love, or whatever, at an accelerated rate. . . ." But I had run out of words, and looking at Emily, it seemed that she had too.

"Good luck with your operation," she said. Then she let out a nervous cough, and handed me a scrap of soggy paper with her phone number. It had been hastily written in a brown eyebrow pencil that was already beginning to smudge. I couldn't figure out when she had the time to do it.

"And you, good luck in your job," I said. I knew it sounded stupid, but after everything that had happened I couldn't think of anything else to add. "I'll call you soon."

"Yes," she said, "I hope so."

I tried to tell if she was just being polite, but couldn't.

"By the way," she asked, "did you ever mention exactly which organ it was you were needing? That way, if I come across a good one. . . ."

"No," I said, "I didn't."

"Well, Paul," and she gave me one of her blushes, "I know at least one that's in pretty good shape."

"Thanks," I said, then shutting the door to the throb of the pool pump, I turned as sharply as I could and left.

It was only on the way home that I realized that I'd forgotten to ask Emily her last name. Or to tell Emily my own.

8

My house, back in those days, was basically a living room, bedroom, bath and kitchen. I rented it furnished, and it came with a couple of pictures — a seascape and one of a man praying — but not much else. It was, I suppose, nothing special. When I returned home I took a long shower to get rid of the salt, confused by what had just happened. The article in Dr. Pearlman's office also claimed that during funerals and in times of war the human body went into a sort of frenzy to reproduce itself. That must be what had gone on amid the elemental stuff at the organ pool, I decided. Why else did people go to horror movies? But had I taken advantage of Emily, or had she, driven wild by her daily exposure to all those primal body parts, been unable to restrain herself, and taken advantage of me?

In any case, I found myself in a surprisingly unsettled state of mind. As usual when this happened, I gave up trying to explain things, and went to bed early, my fuzzy green afghan pulled beneath my chin. I had had the blanket as a boy, and it was far fuzzier now than years ago, mirroring, in a way, the fraying of my beliefs as I grew older. I tried to sleep, moving the radio station from classical ("Liebestode") to oldies ("Love Me Tender") to country and western ("Love Hurts"), but remained awake, so I put on my navy flannel robe with red piping and walked over to the window.

There, to my surprise, beneath the pale yellow light of the streetlamp, were two men I'd never seen before, talking quietly. Both were dressed in brightly colored ski parkas, and wore identical knit woolen caps. They seemed to be friends, and talked in the way friends often do, without looking at each other. Instead each stared out into the darkness as if he were addressing it directly, or maybe only listening. Not that they were speaking all that much, and what was said, naturally, I couldn't hear.

By then it was nearly two in the morning, and it was unusual for people to be out so late in this particular section of St. Nils, so I pulled up a chair. Given my own unsettled state of mind, watching two strangers seemed as good a way to spend my time as any. Behind me, the radio played another country song, and another. An hour passed. Maybe, I decided, two guys hanging around a street corner, even if it was my own corner, weren't so interesting. I made myself a cup of tea — chamomile — and when I returned, the men were still there. Another thirty minutes passed, and the chamomile began to kick in. I yawned. Then a car pulled up, an ancient Buick Roadmaster, the kind with actual portholes in the front fender, plus continents of rust, and oceans of Bondo. It idled noisily next to the two men until the doors opened with a heart-wrenching creak, the men climbed in, and the car limped off into the night. At last, I was ready to sleep.

I left my dirty cup by the window, crawled back into bed, and lay there, but instead of falling asleep, my mind wandered back to a time long ago, when my organ hadn't yet developed those bad spots, back to a time when I was young, and lived on the Broken Record Ranch, with Mom and Dad, and my pony Dominique. Back then, I remembered, every morning my mother would wrap a bologna sandwich with mustard in wax paper, take a couple of apples, a few ripe olives, a croissant, and tuck them all in Dominique's scuffed and fragrant leather saddlebags. Then I'd strap on my chaps, grab my whip, saddle Dominique, and ride off into the hills for a day of play. Sometimes I'd whip her broad haunches, and sometimes she'd take the bit between her teeth and run, her head lowered, through thickets of scrub and forests of cactus with me hanging on for dear life. And eventually, when we stopped, Dominique would wait patiently while I brushed myself off and treated my scratches with the bottle of Mercurochrome that Mom kept tucked in the saddlebags. All that seemed a thousand years ago.

So I lay there in my bed and thought about Dominique, and Emily, and the two strangers, and the Buick that took them away. Then, I guess, I fell asleep.

The next morning I woke curled in the afghan, suprisingly refreshed. I made a pot of coffee, scrambled some eggs and toasted some bread. When I finished breakfast, I washed the plates, and wondered how I would fill up the rest of my day. Outside of my medical chores, there wasn't much to do, and my business as a typewriter repairman, never exactly robust, had dropped to such pitiable levels that I was lucky to take in one job a week. Of course I understood that I had to get a new career, and fast, but the truth was I really loved those old typewriters, and at almost thirty years of age, I wasn't looking forward to any changes.

Fortunately, I remembered the torn slip of paper on which Emily had written her phone number, and so I reached into my closet and fished around in the pocket of my sports coat. If anything, the number had gotten even more smudged by its stay there during the night. I walked to the window, but couldn't make out if the last digit was a 5 or a 3. I decided to take a chance. I would try the 3 first, and then, if that didn't work, I'd try the 5.

As luck had it, the 3 turned out to belong to a carpet cleaning service, which that very week was offering a special: any room in my house for only $19.95. I was about to hang up when I looked around. In truth, my carpet was filthy. It hadn't been cleaned or even vacuumed for as long as I could remember, and in several corners a blue haze was beginning to creep up the walls. I couldn't really afford the luxury of that sort of thing, but if Emily ever did come for a visit, I would have to clean the place up anyway. "Sure," I told the pleasant-sounding woman on the phone. "Why not? When can you do it?"

"This is your lucky day," she said. "It just so happens that one of our skilled technicians is already working in your neighborhood, and he's providing one of your satisfied neighbors the very same special you're about to enjoy." She told me I could expect to hear from this same technician any minute.

Ten minutes later, the doorbell rang and a middle-aged man with "Leo" written in a red oval over the left pocket of his blue work shirt stood in front of me, wheezing. As he wheezed, he rocked slightly from side to side, not like a tall tree exactly, but more like a bush about to topple. And like many a bush, there was something oddly likable about him.

He opened his mouth. "Are you the guy who called about the rug?"

"Why yes," I said, "I am."

I invited him in to look at the damage. "Here's the rug to be cleaned," I explained.

Leo bent down to look it over, and when he straightened up again he made a sad-sounding grunt. He could stand to lose a few pounds and the seat of his pants was shiny. "It's pretty bad," he said, "but I can throw in the special Deep Cleaning treatment or the Stain Guard Protection, a value of fifty dollars, for an extra twenty, bringing your total to $39.95."

"Well thanks," I said. "It does seem like a bargain, but why don't we skip those for now?"

Clearly this Leo was a man used to disappointment. "It's all the same to me," he said. "I'll be finished in about forty minutes, but I have to tell you that you're missing a real deal." Then he headed back to his truck.

Partly because I had nothing better to do, but also because lately I'd gotten out of the habit of going to the garage to palpitate my organ in preparation for the transplant, as Dr. Pearlman had suggested, I followed Leo outside. Dr. Pearlman had demonstrated for me in his office a series of fairly simple exercises that he said, while of no particular benefit, might possibly produce what he called, "miscellaneous collateral benefits."

"You are suffering from a rare form of orgagenic disintegration that's still largely a mystery to modern medical science," Dr. Pearlman had intoned. "Today you're starting with just one organ," and here he put his white smocked arm around my shoulder, "but it doesn't mean that others won't follow, and fast."

I owned no car, in fact I'd never even learned to drive, but though this meant I often had to carry a heavy office-model typewriter three or four miles from the closest bus stop, it was one of the ways I got by on my slim earnings as a typewriter repairman. The result was that, along with my rented house, I also found myself in possession of a vacant garage, and though there was no actual medical reason that I needed to use that particular location to palpitate my organ, it seemed better, more clinical somehow, than using the place where I lived and slept. It kept the personal problem I was having a little distance from my professional life.

In any case, it was a beautiful day. The birds were yelling overhead, and the corner mailbox, with its new coat of red, white, and blue paint, stood out as crisply in the bright sunlight as a package of breakfast cereal. Leo's truck, I observed, was dented, and there were strips of gray duct tape holding the bumpers in place. Leo was not, it seemed, getting rich in this business, and I began to feel guilty that I hadn't agreed to the Stain Guard Special, even if he had taken his rejection so well. Forty minutes later I had completed the exercises for my organ and returned to the house in time to see Leo hauling a large machine with tubing protruding from its sides back to his truck. Leo moved slowly, not so much as if he was very tired, but as if he had nothing better to do. Several times he just stopped in the middle of the sidewalk, and sighed.

"Do you have time for a cup of coffee?" I said.

Leo's broad face, tired as it was, or appeared to be but wasn't, brightened. "Sure," he said. "I don't have another job scheduled for a while."

"Come on in," I said, and I felt better. So there we were: two guys with basically nothing better to do sitting at the kitchen table, one telling the other stories of carpet cleaning and the things a person can find beneath a rug. Leo seemed excited to relay this information, but underneath it all, I could still detect a certain sadness. Whatever was bothering him was more than just his job, I guessed, and many of Leo's stories seemed to have an underlying theme of people who put on a brave front for strangers.

Leo picked up his coffee mug and held it between his hands. "I can't imagine a greater honor and a privilege to be invited into so many people's homes," he said. "No matter how many times I do it, it still fills me with awe to be able to share my clients' most private secrets, to earn their trust as I go from room to room, moving their furniture, at times even having the drawers of their bedside tables slide open to reveal the intimate details of lives: the kinky photographs, the bizarre pieces of sex equipment, the groveling letters to celebrities they've never sent, the unpaid bills from expensive department stores that they've kept hidden from their spouses." His coffee sloshed around in its cup a bit.

"Imagine," Leo continued, "being able to access, in a way that only a trained observer can, the very secrets a person believes to be 'harmless' or else hidden safely away. Hidden, but of course in places utterly predictable to anyone who has had experience with this kind of thing: places which, in effect, scream out to be exposed by the sort of professional who knows their true meaning. That scrap of paper by your phone, for example, with the number almost the same as mine that's written in what looks like smudged eyebrow pencil, I'll bet there's some story there, right?" Then he stopped, almost as if he was frightened by what he had said. "Excuse me. I didn't mean to get personal." He shook his head. "You know," he said, "sometimes the responsibility is just too much. The burden is too heavy. Not in your case, of course, but there are times when I think I'd just rather say no to all of this power."

Leo carefully lowered his coffee cup and stared into the corners of my kitchen, as if peering into its secrets. Then he shook his head, bitterly this time. "By the way, that stain in the living room rug looks like a real bad one. I could barely make a dent in it."

"What stain?" I said, and got up and followed Leo to the

next room. I had to say I didn't remember any particular stain, but then the entire rug had been in such a complete state of distress that it was entirely probable I hadn't noticed it. Cleaned, the room looked much larger, and the vanilla scent of whatever he had used to take out the dirt was pleasant, but I could see that he was right. In one corner of the room was a lightish rectangle, with the narrow top (or bottom, depending upon which direction you were standing) rounded off into a graceful arc. It looked (again, depending on the angle it was viewed) either like one of those early space capsules designed to land their precious cargo of astronauts safely in the ocean, or like a nipple of a baby bottle.

We returned to the kitchen, where Leo meandered his way to the sink and rinsed out his cup. "Thanks," he said. "You can't imagine how important it is for me to keep up human contact these days." He shook my hand.

Then he left me alone again. I sat for a while, listening to the sound of his truck's faulty muffler being gradually absorbed by silence, before I walked back to the living room. Leo had forgotten to return the furniture to where it was supposed to be, and so for the next several minutes, I did that. When I was finished, I tried the 5 that Emily had written, but got one of those answering machine greetings that only said the number, so I left a message: "Uh, I'm the guy you met at the pool the other day," followed by my own phone number. It was lame, yes, but I didn't want to get too personal, just in case that second number was also wrong.

The next morning I tried again and left another message. Then, every hour or so, I tried again, though I knew enough to hang up before I got the machine. I didn't want Emily to think that she had attracted an obsessive maniac or anything. In between calls, I imagined her at her work, bobbing up and down in that light blue two-piece bathing suit. Then, after spitting on the plate of her facemask so it won't fog up, she adjusts its straps. Next, she secures the rubber mouthpiece firmly to her lips, and looks around, brushing lightly against the organs clustered around her as, treading water, she turns her body in the pool. But wait! Her sharp eyes spot something at the bottom of the deep end. She dives, a spleen, or maybe a lung, has died during the night, and she brings it up, cupped to her chest, careful not to frighten the other organs. "Good-bye," she whispers, as she carries it to the big blue trash can, lifts the lid, and carefully lowers it to its eternal rest.

In between my calling Emily and thinking about Emily, I walked out to the back porch to jiggle the vat of typewriter solvent that contained an old Smith Corona that the lady next door had left for me to fix. She had kept it, she said, in her kitchen to type out her recipes, and as a result it was thick with grease and oregano, the aftermath of a bad spill. I had taken out the ribbon and then dropped the whole thing in the vat to soak. In a couple days, when most of the ink and grease had softened and dropped away, I would take a brush to its mechanism.

I had begun my career as a typewriter repairman many years earlier, while I was still a boy, and my teacher had been an old Dutch perfectionist, who, before he would agree to pronounce me competent, forced me to take apart and reassemble, blindfolded, an Underwood office model. Maybe it was the ter-

17

rorist syndrome, but the Underwood was still one of my favorites, along with those ancient portables with curiously cigar-sounding names, the Olivettis, Smith Coronas, Remingtons and Royals. Even years later there was no more satisfying sound than the smack of a well-placed key on a sheet of twenty-four-pound bond paper. It was like the thump of a ball in a catcher's mitt, imprinting once and for all a single letter, the beginning of (and sometimes, as in the case of "a" and "I") an entire living word, a part of the human mind, onto a page. There were professional typists, of course, whose sounds, unlike my own pedestrian clomps, were more like those of tap dancers or thigh-slapping, lederhosen-clad peasants, but none of those professionals ever affected me in the same way.

At the time I'm speaking of, I worked mostly on electrics, of course. Though I never really enjoyed their irritating hum, as if the typist were at a crowded lunch counter with someone standing at his or her back, that person breathing through his or her congested nasal passages, waiting for the typist to finish up his or her BLT. Naturally, I fixed the electrics, but still believed that, like the higher forms of calligraphic art, a well-typed letter on an old manual typewriter, the impression of each keystroke dark and even, without erasures or hesitation, would one day be a collector's item.

But at least those busybody electrics had provided employment, and were not the faceless, silicon-chip infested wise guys who were replacing them: computers. Writing had been writing back in the old days, and the new word on the street was "word-processing," a phrase that seemed better suited to a cow, or other ruminant. As a result of this general unwillingness to succumb to the trumpets of the march of progress, I spent ever more time idle.

After a lunch of boiled cabbage, which Dr. Pearlman had told me that he had heard was sometimes beneficial in cases like mine, and at the worst couldn't hurt, I rinsed my dishes and opened a window to help dispel the odor. Then I went to the garage, where I fit in an extra session of organ palpitation to make up for those I'd missed the previous day, when I'd been with Emily. When I returned to the house, the place still smelled bad, so instead of trying to phone Emily again, which had been my intention, I opened another window, turned on a small fan, and decided to take a little walk.

In case you've never been to St. Nils, you might want to know that it's a place of mixed Mediterranean climate (average high 70, average low 50), situated on the western coast of the North American continent, with a combination of pine and deciduous forest, largely cut down. Fauna includes rabbits, opossum, coyote and deer. Part of the year the grass is brown, and the rest of the time it's green. The day I'm describing, it was in-between green and brown.

I passed the bakery, the laundry, the pet shop, and the Treasure Chest, where I studied an overpriced, though well-maintained, portable Olivetti chained to a stand in front. Some-times I had bought machines at the Treasure Chest in the past, and after cleaning them, sold them at a small profit, but this had just been put out, and was certain to be marked down. Also, it was a little heavy to carry right at that moment.

When I returned from this walk, as brief as it was, the message on my own answering machine said, "Hi Paul! This is Emily. I'll be out of town for a few days. I'll call you when I get back," and was followed by a dial tone. Emily, I thought, and then suddenly I became frightened. Suppose that by the time she returned to town and we got together she was no longer the person I remembered. So, to be sure my memory would be fresh the next time I met her, I spent the afternoon thinking about her. From 1:30 to 2:30 I recalled how the taste of the dried salt from Emily's skin reminded me of the pretzels I ate as a boy. The pretzels came in sticks, and were sold in glass containers, and I would usually buy one or two each day on the way home from school. They cost a nickel, but the combination of the salt and mustiness seemed to me now a foretaste of an adult and private flavor.

From 2:30 to 3:15, I remembered the paradoxical feel of Emily's coarse and yet also tender hair below the line of her swimsuit, and decided that in many ways it resembled the artificial grass in the Easter baskets that my mother and I would prepare the night before that holiday, staying up late into the night to dye eggs from our own chickens in vinegary reds, blues, and yellows. Then we would hide them in various locations around the ranch — in feed bins and tool boxes for example — and the next morning, like two alcoholic serial killers, pretend that it hadn't been us who'd hidden them, but the Easter Bunny.

From 3:15 to 3:30, I visualized the straining pink tip of Emily's tongue, and how it would poke out shyly and defiantly between her nearly clenched, and slightly yellowed, smoker's teeth. Once out, it would shout its incomprehensible language of pleasure and then, startled by such boldness, beat a quick retreat back to its enamel den behind those two red luscious lips.

From 3:30 to 4:10, I replayed each of those afore-shouted nonsense syllables, each vowel, each urgent grunt, cluck and oof, and, I have to say, I also wondered, as anyone might in a similar exercise testing the power of recollection, how many of them she had actually grunted, uttered or spoken, and how many I had reconstructed out of a combination of memory, hope, and a little water in my left ear at the time, which made it hard for me to understand exactly what she was saying. Was I beginning to obsess? Yes, perhaps I was, I thought, but on the other hand, it seemed important to reconstruct my earliest images of her as solidly as possible because they would be, I knew, the building blocks of the relationship that would last my entire life.

From 4:10 to about 5:30, I thought about how the saline in the pool, as it dried on Emily's skin, made it look as if she had been sprayed with diamond dust mixed with Valspar varnish. I thought about how the tips of Emily's fingers and her toes, wrinkled from all that time in the water, looked like the faces of sleeping babies. I thought about Emily's slight cough, and how she would discreetly turn her head to one side as she quietly swallowed the phlegm it had produced, and hoped she could quit smoking soon, because, as a heavy smoker myself for many years until rising cigarette prices forced me to abandon the habit, I knew firsthand how difficult it was to give up any addiction, but especially smoking. Then, at about 5:35, it was time for my supper.

That evening I prepared another quarter of the cabbage, this time adding a handful of baked lentils, which Dr. Pearlman had said were "completely pointless" in a case as advanced as mine. "But they're cheap," he added, "and full of protein." Then I finished the dishes, paced for a while, and thought about calling Emily, in case she had somehow cut short her plans and returned early, but in the end, thought better of it. I turned on the television, which, oddly, seemed not to work ever since Leo had moved it to clean the carpet underneath. At last, temporarily having run out of things to remember about Emily, although I was pretty sure I could come up with more if I pushed it, I occupied myself by staring out the window. In the twilight, people walked their dogs, or jogged, and kids went by on bicycles. Then, possibly from all the tension of the day, or all the fresh air I had inhaled during my earlier walk, I fell asleep.

When I woke it was dark, and I was surprised to see that the same pair of men from two nights ago had returned. Or at least I supposed they were the same. I couldn't absolutely be sure, because on this, the second night, one had made himself into a kind of bench by dropping to his hands and knees, and the other, who was the same person as the night before, was sitting on his back, and waiting. Every so often the seated man said something, and I presumed there was an answer, because the sitter would crank his head slightly toward the one on whom he was sitting. I couldn't make out any words. They both were wearing heavy winter clothing, and the one who had made himself into a bench was wearing heavy boots, as if for hiking. The other guy wore tennis shoes.

So the men continued, waiting in the cold and the dark, chatting in this peculiar way for nearly an hour. At last, at about 2:30 in the morning, the same car as on the previous evening, the Roadmaster, pulled up. Both men got in, and, with a loud clunking of doors, the car drove creakily off.

I remained there in the dark, staring out the window, waiting for something else to happen, but nothing did. Suddenly, I recalled how, after Emily had pulled her bathing suit back on, while she was reaching in back to hook the top by herself, she had grown mysteriously quiet, as if she were engaged in some philosophical speculation. She had even looked off in the distance, brushing my hand away when I attempted to touch her. Then she got up and walked over to check the pool thermometer. When she'd finished, she came back to where I was waiting on a coil of hose.

"Sometimes," Emily had said, "it seems as if we're all only candles burning, and the brighter our light shines, the closer we find ourselves to completely burning up. Sometimes," she had said, "our wax drips down, then after it ruins the finish of the table top, it continues right down to the floor, where it creates the kind of stain you can never get rid of." Her voice had dropped there, as if she were ashamed, and she blushed.

"And sometimes, especially if the candle has been placed too close to the edge of the table, and an animal, usually in my experience a cat, knocks against it so that the candle actually topples, it sets the whole place on fire, the table, rugs, and everything. Everything goes up in smoke, and often there's the loss of human life as well — a mother or father, maybe even a child — and for what? For a little extra light? So you can read a book when you should be sleeping? To have a romantic evening with a steak and soft music? To heat some chaffing dish that's bound to get cold in any case?" Then she said a couple words that were drowned out by the noise of the pool pump, which had just kicked on.

"Excuse me," I started to say.

She stopped and stared at me, as if she'd just been awakened from a dream. "Oh!" she'd said. "I forgot. I shouldn't be talking like this, what with your organ and all."

And so I returned to dozing in my armchair, still placed

before the now-empty stage of my window. The following day, I resolved, I would try to remember more facts that demonstrated Emily's talents as a philosopher and a thinker.

In the morning light, my rug looked particularly good, but curiously, the stain, formerly nearly unnoticeable, suddenly seemed to dominate the entire room. Was it just having it pointed out to me that seemed to exaggerate its importance? I would have to ask Emily, I thought; this was her kind of question. Meanwhile, I wondered if there was some special cleaning compound I could use to treat it, or if there was anything else I could do short of eventually replacing the rug. I tried to recall what caused it in the first place. If I could remember what I'd dropped down there, I reasoned, then possibly I could get it out before Emily arrived. But at that moment I could come up with absolutely nothing.

For breakfast I had another quarter of the head of cabbage, a brioche, pineapple juice, and coffee, as I pored over the daily paper for hints of new medical discoveries that might apply to my case. It was a discouraging process, for not only did any promising treatment tend to be overstated, but those that were credible generally took from five to ten years to appear on the market. Even with the intercession of Dr. Pearlman, it would no doubt be months at the very earliest, before I could get enrolled in one of those promising pilot studies, assuming I could even find one.

Suddenly, just as I was finishing my second cup of coffee, looking at the bottom of the cup trying to decide whether or not to drink down the spongy mess of crumbs that was the result of a piece of brioche falling in, I was overwhelmed by yet another unbidden image of Emily. This time she had replaced her swimsuit, and, whether out of modesty or finality, had wrapped the pink towel around her narrow waist as she walked with me, fully clothed, toward the door.

"When I was young," Emily had said, "I had a spotted dog that we would tie up to a pole in our backyard to keep her from following us whenever we left the house. It wasn't that she was so devoted, really, and we weren't so crazy about her — she was a biter, and had already gotten a few of my friends, some pretty badly — but it was just that she couldn't stand to be left behind.

"Well, that dog would bark and pull, and bark and pull so hard against that rope that when we'd return home a couple hours or a couple days later, we'd find her completely passed out from lack of oxygen. Her name was Miss Mary Dog, and though my mother said she'd outgrow the habit she never did. Finally, after about four years of this, the rope broke, and she must have run after us onto the freeway because a man who witnessed the accident she caused said he'd never seen a dog so worried.

"I only bring this up now," Emily had said, "because I just hope I don't find myself getting attached to you that way. If I did, I don't know what would happen."

II

It wasn't until over a whole week had passed following my visit to the organ pool, that I realized that in my excitement of meeting Emily, I had forgotten to pick out an organ. I felt like a complete fool, and to make matters worse, clearly, because Dr. Pearlman had gone to such great lengths to obtain permission for me to make my visit, I couldn't possibly ask him again. And suppose I could, what excuse could I possibly put forward?

Plus, I thought, even if by some astronomical chance Dr. Pearlman did, say, all on his own, suggest a second visit in case the first hadn't worked out, how would Emily feel? Would she think that I was taking advantage of the precious spontaneity of our first encounter and was now arranging for a repeat performance? Would she believe that I expected this sort of thing on a regular basis, any time I just happened to feel like dropping in at her workplace? In short, would Emily feel wooed or pursued? I couldn't be certain, but for me the entire wonder of our earlier encounter had lain completely in the uncensored generosity of Emily's passion. It was a sort of a not-to-be-re-peated encounter that I hoped one day we would tell our grand-children about as they were seated around some groaning Thanksgiving or birthday table, when one of them, maybe little Vanessa, would ask how the two of us had met. "It's an odd story," I would begin, and Emily would blush. So I knew it was imperative that I leave the question of our future "relationship" where it belonged: in Emily's small, wet, strong hands.

Besides, even if I did drop in completely unannounced, and explained to her that this time, no matter how much she desired me, her strong feelings of a personal nature would have to be held in check, how could I possibly make such an impor-tant decision as picking out an organ in the agitated state I would undoubtedly be in? Dr. Pearlman, no doubt not wishing to in-cur blame if his choice had been a wrong one, had merely told me to "trust your instincts," and to pick one that "speaks to you." Yet I had never actually seen my own ailing organ ("show-ing you the X rays would only upset you more," Dr. Pearlman had said), so even if I did manage to stay calm, how could I compare an organ still in my body to one parked outside of it when I had no idea what to look for?

But could I learn? I understood, of course, from other experiences in my life that appearances could fool a person, and that a manic personality was often just the hard, brittle shell of a soft, depressive nutmeat, but was this also true for organs? It was possible that having been raised without the painful neces-sity to present, as I do myself, an outward face to the public in order to appear "normal" and "reliable," that an organ might somehow escape the double-faced standard that confuses so many of us in everyday life. Maybe all organs were by nature without prevarication, and to pick out a good one by looks alone would be a snap. Maybe if I'd paid more attention to the medical aspects of my visit that afternoon at the pool, instead of you-know-what, at that very second I'd be on my way to a full recovery.

I spent a sleepless night over this problem, along with fiddling with the television to try to make it work. I could get only half the screen at any given time, and the halves constantly changed around, so that one minute I'd be watching a couple kissing, and then find myself staring at their feet. By morning, I decided that I would just tell a fib. I'd tell Dr. Pearlman that I never had exactly got to the pool at all on that day. I'd instead explain that there was a problem with the bus, and when I'd thought about it I'd decided to leave the choice of a suitable organ entirely in his capable hands. My reasoning here was that such an unsolicited testimonial as this might spur Dr. Pearlman either into insisting that I try again, or even that he might go himself and use his expertise to choose a really great organ. But in this latter scenario, I realized he would meet Emily, and then what would happen? Would there be a repeat of the encounter Emily and I had earlier, but this time with a partner who could more easily afford to support her in style? Was I getting jealous? I'm afraid I was.

For breakfast I had a reprise of the previous day's, plus a dollop of cabbage, and was rinsing my dishes when these ignoble thoughts, as painful as they were, were interrupted by the sound of a doorbell. Could it be Emily home from her trip, I thought wildly for a moment. But opening the door, who should I find standing there but Leo, broad, short, and grinning. Even though it was early in the day, there were still sweat stains under Leo's yawning armpits.

I was taken aback, just a bit. "Leo," I said, "it's good to see you, but why are you here so unexpectedly? Did you leave some important tool or piece of equipment behind? Couldn't you at least have telephoned first?"

Then it was Leo's turn to look surprised. "Not at all," he said. "I am here in answer to your call."

"What? Huh? Me? How? When?"

Leo explained that at sometime during the middle of the previous night someone had phoned. It had been a man, Leo told me, who seemed very upset. He was worried about a stain in a rug Leo had recently cleaned, and in the midst of several pointed threats, he asked Leo if there was any way to clean or bleach it. The man hadn't left an address or a phone number. "I just assumed it was you," Leo said.

I assured him it was not. Curiously however, I went on to tell Leo, I *had* been thinking nearly identical thoughts about the stain in my own carpet. "So if you've got a second," I said, "I'd be very happy if you could take a moment to look at it."

Leo eyed me peculiarly for a minute, as if he was figuring out the solution to a difficult math problem in a foreign language. Then, as he had evidently reached it, an expression of relief washed over his broad face. He took my hand and pumped it up and down.

"It *was* a strange phone call," he said, "but now that I'm here, I'm glad to be needed. Even better, Paul — I hope you don't mind if I call you by your first name — I'm happy to hear you say it wasn't you who made it. Last night, when I thought it was you, Paul, it bothered me. I thought, 'Here it is the middle of the night, and Paul isn't happy with the cleaning job you did, Leo.' So I tried to sleep, but I couldn't, and I lay there, hour after hour, thinking, 'Why would Paul do something like this? Why would Paul say these terrible things?' Then after a while, I figured it out. I finally understood that your calling me at that hour of the night, screaming those threats over the phone (of course I know now it wasn't you, but I thought it was you at the time), far from being just bad behavior, was in fact an accolade of trust and confidence. After thinking for a while I finally figured out what happened. And here it is:

"What happened was you woke. You got up for a glass of water. You turned on the light, and then you saw the stain. You drank the water, and tried to sleep, but you couldn't. 'That Leo,' you said to yourself. 'I know he stands behind his work because I can see the honesty in his eyes. I know he's a big man, but how big is he? I know he's a fair man, but how fair is he? Now here it is, 3:30 in the morning, and I wonder if he is big enough to accept a little criticism any time of the day or night. Sure, there are plenty of people who will hear things in the light of day, and maybe even promise to correct them, but I wonder how my friend Leo will take being woken in the middle of the night. And then, just for fun, if he gets through that part of it why don't I really give him a test? Why don't I threaten him a little while I'm at it, and scream, too, just to see how big Leo is, as well as honest? Why don't I,' you said, 'just give old Leo a call right now?'

"And so you did, but then, when Leo turned out to be both big and fair, you were surprised. You said, 'Here it is, 3:30 in the morning, and I have acted like an asshole because I doubted Leo. Leo is so big and so fair, that now I am embarrassed to leave my name, because although I now know he is big and fair, I still don't know if he's big and fair enough to not be angry and not to take revenge on me for having woken him up. Big enough and fair enough not to write "Home of an Asshole" in weed killer on the pitiful piece of front lawn that I call my own, or spray the same in purple paint on my front door while I'm fast asleep. Or maybe even call a pizza delivery place and order a dozen large pepperonis, or call the Mafia guy Leo just happens to know and to have him rough me up a bit.' But as you can see I'm not angry. Leo is not angry. As you can see, I'm right here, and I want you to know Leo is not the kind of person to hold a grudge, or anything like that, but instead, as you can see, Paul, I respect you for being able to open up your feelings to me. In fact, I'm really sorry you now claim it wasn't you who called."

I looked at Leo more closely. He *did* look tired, and what I'd decided was probably depression, possibly even a form of incipient mental illness, appeared to be no more than the result of a lack of sleep, because it seemed clear that, after being awoken in the middle of the night by god-knows-what sort of crank, Leo had probably been unable to go back to sleep. Insomnia: I myself had had problems with the condition that very same night, and it was possible that some unidentified atmospheric phenomenon was to blame. I looked at Leo again, and saw that the latter's small eyes were actually filling with tears.

Leo wiped his nose on his sleeve. "It's surprisingly rare that a carpet cleaner is given such a chance to enter into another person's life," he said. "Certain things in my life of late have made such an act as yours more important than mere money." Then he seized my hand from where it had been resting by my side and shook it. He blinked to keep the water from completely filling his eyes, pulled out a large crumpled handkerchief, blew his nose with surprising force, and pumped my hand again, still holding the handkerchief.

Practically out of nowhere I was reminded of the first time I met Emily, that moment I had just held out my hand for her to shake. I'd been standing there at the edge of the pool, and Emily still was wearing her scuba gear. She removed her mask to get a better look at me; it left behind two red rings along the bottoms of her cheeks. Perhaps it was my imagination, but she seemed to blush then, even as she shivered slightly from the breeze that came through the open roof.

"Is it so hard to shake my hand?" I had asked.

She removed the scuba mouthpiece from between her lips and spoke, I thought, with remarkable candor considering that as far as I knew, she'd never seen me before in her entire life.

"When I was growing up," Emily explained, "my parents, Brad and Lonnie, cautioned me about shaking the hands of strangers. Now," she continued, "even though I've grown older, I'm still torn by the simultaneous display of power and vulnerability implied in that one seemingly simple act so important to the well-being of society. In other words, does the power of the act of shaking hands consist in our grasping a hand that otherwise might do us harm, or is it in the vulnerability of presenting our own hand to a stranger and letting that person move it around as if it wasn't ours in the first place?"

I didn't think that she was expecting an answer, so I kept quiet. Her own hands remained at her side.

Then Emily had turned away to fool with a buckle on her scuba weights. "These things get really slippery," she said.

While I was recalling this, Leo remained waiting at the front door. "Oh," I said. "I'm afraid my mind wandered for a minute. Come in. I've got a pot of coffee on the stove, plus a little warm brioche. If you like raw cabbage, you're welcome to a bowl of that too, it's a thing I'm doing right now."

Leo, as it turned out, displayed a surprising appetite for raw cabbage as well as brioche, and it was nearly noon by the time he wiped his mouth on his sleeve, rose from the kitchen table, put his few dishes in the sink, walked back to the table, wiped his mouth again, walked away carrying his napkin, looked for the trash container, found it, tossed the napkin in, and said, "Time to get back to work. You don't happen to know the actual origin of the stain, do you, Paul?"

I confessed that by a strange coincidence I'd been thinking about that very problem at about three that very morning myself, but had come to no conclusions.

Leo studied me warily for a moment. He opened his mouth as if to speak, then apparently changed his mind. He paused. "No matter," he finally said. "A surprising amount of the time people are wrong anyway."

Leo opened a bag he brought with him, and fished out a kit with several small vials and a package of Q-tips. "I call this my stain detective," he said, then he dipped each of the tips into a different vial, and straightening up, he walked to the window, and studied the swabs in the light, mumbling from time to time under his breath. I could tell he was a craftsman; he was in no hurry to rush to a conclusion.

I waited for a minute, and then another, and then, when Leo showed no sign of movement, I exited to do the dishes. I filled the sink with liquid detergent and swirled it around so that it would distribute itself evenly. Exactly when did the stain in the rug first appear? I wasn't sure, but it could well be that this whole organ business was affecting my memory in addition to everything else. I remembered that once I had left a box of typewriter ribbons somewhere in the house for a few months, and moved them to the garage when they began to leak, and then someone stole them, but I couldn't be sure of the exact spot.

On the other hand, I thought, practicing for just the sort of philosophical conversation it was clear I might expect to have one day soon with Emily, what *was* a stain? Merely a variant of color in a fabric that in itself was a variant of an earth full of a whole variety of colors. "Glory be to God for damaged things," a poet whose name I couldn't recall once put it, for what was memory but a stain on the pure field of our consciousness, and who did we think we were, to remove a spot from such a picture? If you looked at the Old Masters, I thought, you would see how intensely disappointing they were once some well-meaning curator sent them out for a cleaning. And wasn't every human fingerprint also a stain, and every digression in a life the stain that literally defined the life itself? Of course they were. And were not our words themselves a stain on the blank page of possibility, and to speak therefore to shatter the stainless silence of the world? Hmm, I hummed.

Then . . . what did that "Hmm" remind me of? Was it the exact moment that Emily and I were sitting atop a pile of crumbling blue Styrofoam kickboards which must have been left over from the pool's recreational past? Emily was facing me, and I her, as we rubbed each other's shoulders and stared silently into our reflections in the pupils of each other's eyes. "Hmm," Emily had sighed, and then she began to speak.

"My first period," Emily had said as her voice dropped lower, "came on one of those winter nights so cold I'd crawl into my bed, still wearing the green mukluks my mother had knitted. They were scratchy but warm, and I've always had a tendency toward cold feet, probably a result of my unusually low blood pressure. At any rate, I pulled back the immense white mountain of the polyester comforter Lonnie had personally stuffed, revealing the cold, white expanse of the sheets themselves. Then I slid in, the icy fabric prickling the backs of my thighs as the flannel nightgown my mother had sewn as a present for my twelfth birthday rode up nearly to the twin creases of my girlish buttocks. I grabbed the fabric firmly in each hand and slid it back down again."

Emily stopped rubbing my shoulders for a moment and began to hum a little song. "What's going on here?" I remember thinking. "Who is this woman I met only moments ago who speaks to me as if I should be privy to the most intimate details in her life? Does she tell me these things because she knows we already have a special bond, or does she tell these things to everyone? And even supposing she does tell such details to every Tom, Dick and Harry, does that mean I should treat this information as somehow less valuable?"

Then she resumed rubbing, and, as if the very motion of her hands was kneading her words out of my muscles, continued. "Back then," she said, "I didn't know quite what to make of it, except that everything — the chill, the short intake of breath as my legs touched the sheets, and the subsequent long, relieved exhalation into the already frosty air of my bedroom — was strangely exciting. Nor had I been prepared for the double shock awaiting me the next morning: the first when I saw my sheets, formerly so white, now stained with the nascent gush of my womanhood, and the second, when I looked outside my bedroom window to check on how my pet mallard, Mr. Quackers, was doing after such an unusually cold night. And there he was, his body frozen fast to the surface of the pond, his neck chewed off during the night by a fox who had apparently visited him while he had been held in place by the ice, quacking no doubt pathetically for help that never came, quacking for me. But instead that morning there was no more Mr. Quackers. There was only an eaten-away bowl in the shape of a duck, like one of those giant tostada shells you leave behind after you've finished all the tomato and shredded lettuce and guacamole inside, sitting in the middle of a pool of blood." Emily grimaced, then sighed, then grimaced again. "I loved Mr. Quackers," she said. "I hope all this doesn't upset you."

At that moment, standing there in my kitchen, I could scarcely wait to see her again. And when I did, I would say, "No Emily, it only makes me love you more." I heard a cough from about a foot behind my ear. I drained the dishwater and turned to see Leo standing there, holding out a brown clipboard. "It looks like I'll have to order some special stain-dissolving chemicals," Leo said. "They should be here in a week or so. I'll give you a call when they come in. I've got to go now, Paul, but I sure have enjoyed spending the morning with you, even if it wasn't you who called."

"Not at all, Leo," I said. "The pleasure has been mine." I added that I was sorry that someone, though certainly not me, had kept Leo up all night, and that it might not be a bad idea for him to knock off early and see if he could get some rest.

"I don't know," Leo said. "These days I try to stay as busy as possible." Then he lurched gently and majestically toward my front door, his blue work pants somehow heartbreaking in their bagginess. Watching Leo as he shambled out over the uneven bricks of my front sidewalk to his battered truck, I thought more about my earlier theory that there was something more than mere sleeplessness to Leo. There was also something melancholy, and possibly degradingly servile and tragic. Perhaps it was the result of having a profession that required a person to spend so much time on his hands and knees. Yet I had known one or two rug cleaners in the past who were extroverted, cheerful whistlers, even headstrong, vicious optimists, so Leo's profession alone didn't explain everything.

Later that night, as I sat in my chair by the window, I wondered if the two mysterious men would come again. My familiar corner, suddenly deprived of its loiterers, seemed bereft: a streetlight shining on nothing, an empty stage, its actors out on an equity dispute, or maybe just playing cards during the intermission. After a long three hours during which no one at all showed up, I decided to turn on the television, but remembered I had forgotten to mention to Leo that he probably had broken it. I shook it a few times, hoping some loose circuit might pop back into place, but it did not, so I gave up and opened the *Journal of Amateur Anthropology*.

The entire issue was dedicated to documenting an obscure Indonesian tribe whose religion required its elders to go out each night to the hills that surrounded their village. Once there, the men built small fires and awaited the arrival of someone or something — it was unclear to the scholar/writers if it was a god or merely some low-level technological advance that the natives believed would help them to better organize their lives. The article was accompanied by various photographs, taken under poor light conditions, of men sitting around their fires and chatting. Curiously, a few of the participants were resting on their hands and knees, while others of the tribe used them as benches. Who these men were, and why they did this, the anthropologists were unable to discover. It also was unclear whether to be designated as a bench was an honor, a punishment, or just a form of social courtesy.

And then, all these thoughts about chairs brought back yet another memory. I suddenly remembered how, at one point in our encounter, Emily and I had found ourselves atop the rickety, peeling, eight-foot-tall lifeguard chair. From that vantage point the organ pool below looked something like a painting by Paul Klee (or was it Miro?). It was odd, I thought, suddenly sitting in my own chair once again, how time, even as little as the three days since I had seen Emily, had begun to blunt and compress the inventory of my memory, even as in our larger lives one year blurs into the next, and one modernist abstract painter becomes another.

Then I was transported back to the pool once again, atop that other, wobbling chair, and Emily chose that very moment to seize a strand of my hair and twist it around her finger to wring out the salty water.

"Ouch," I told her as the chair creaked beneath the two of us. "That is really uncomfortable. Can you possibly stop?"

To my amazement Emily's features changed. Her eyes turned inward. She bit her lip, sucked in her cheeks, and her nostrils pinched themselves shut. Her breathing became shallow and rapid. Then she snapped out of it. "I'm sorry," she said. "I kind of lost track of where I was, and for some reason I fell back into a time when I was growing up, when on summer evenings our house was often surrounded by stern-faced men, standing in groups of twos and threes, smoking cigars." She let drop the part of my hair she'd been wrapping around her finger.

I assured her I didn't mind her drifting off, that I'd been known to do it myself, but the hair business had started to get painful.

"I'm really sorry, " Emily said, "but let me continue. At first I thought this was more or less normal. Believe it or not, I thought that all over Minnesota, at about eight at night every house was surrounded by men, puffing away, although it was true I had never actually heard anyone talk about it. Then one day in the second grade, when I was on my first sleepover, I asked my friend, a little blond girl with a sty in her left eye, where the men with the cigars were that night, and what she thought had delayed them. My friend looked at me strangely. 'Are you nuts?' she lisped."

Emily blushed. "Little by little, as I visited the homes of my other friends and saw no sign of the men, I became curious as to who they were. When I asked Brad and Lonnie they would immediately change the subject, or pretend not to hear. As you can well imagine, the result of this kind of response was that cigar-smoking strangers began to dominate my reveries, and even my dreams."

Emily told me she never actually found out what these men were doing there. When she persisted with questions to her parents, she only received vague replies, such as they must be a part of some government study, or they had something to do with national defense, because everyone was very concerned about the Communists in those days. They disappeared, Emily said, when she left her home for college, and now, she said, she couldn't be positive they even ever existed.

"What did the men look like?" I asked.

"Oh, about the same as any white middle-aged men smoking big cigars," she said, "completely ridiculous. Except that even on the hottest, most humid evenings of summer, they all wore parkas and a ton of other winter gear. I guess it was supposed to be a disguise."

I put down the *Journal of Amateur Anthropology*, and began to flip aimlessly through one of the holiday gift catalogues that I kept meaning to throw out, but hadn't had the time to. Those men, outside my house the other night, and those natives, thousands of miles away, both engaged in the same, mysterious and oddly tender habits. . . . A feeling I was quite unused to slipped over me, of inexplicable peace, as if for the first time in my life there might be a plan, a synchronicity somewhere behind this world which, though it had eluded me thus far, might one day be knowable. I could feel my organ begin to relax, and it was in exactly that mood that I arose from my armchair to ascertain who was knocking on my front door that late at night.

It was two men. Was it the same pair who had been out there that previous night? I couldn't tell. Tonight however, the taller of the two was wearing a tasseled knit cap of red and white fine gauge wool with a diamond pattern and a border of small diamonds on the bottom, a pair of cat's eye sunglasses with side shields to protect himself from snow glare (even though there was no snow), a yellow and black mountain guide parka, waterproof insulated pants, black gloves, pile-lined snow boots, and aluminum snowshoes. His partner had a visored cap with earflaps and the identical cat's eye, glare-blocking sunglasses. He wore, however, a solid red parka with his black, waterproof, insulated pants, but the same boots and snowshoes. His gloves were yellow, with a black wrist strap to adjust the tension, and black, non-slip palms. Standing there at my threshold, the men both stamped their feet a few times, as if to knock off any imaginary snow. They were sweating rather heavily.

"I saw your light on," the taller one said. "Do you suppose that we can use your phone for an emergency? It's a local call."

"Sure," I said. It seemed unlikely that they were burglars. They removed their snowshoes and leaned them outside against the brick by the door. I pointed to the phone on its table, and they both walked over to it, the shorter one dialing, the taller standing between the phone and me as if to block out any conversation I might overhear. The man did not have to worry; my swimmer's ear had gotten worse, and though I wasn't sure how this was medically possible, it appeared to be spreading to the other side of my head. I wondered if there was some special chemical in the organ pool water I should know about. I made a note to mention it to Emily when she returned.

The strangers finished their call and apologized for any inconvenience. Then they headed back outside, tucked their snowshoes under their arms, and disappeared into the night, this time not waiting by the streetlight, but continuing past it into the darkness. I was left completely puzzled. I walked back over to my chair and sank down, idly picking up an ancient L. L. Bean Holiday Gift Catalogue, the one for 1998. There, to my utter amazement, tucked away among the winterwear, were the very same two men who had just used my phone.

What could I do? I stared down into the fibers of my clean carpet. They were long and loose, a brownish green, the kind called a "shag." From out of the corner of my eye, the stain seemed to be coming back. Suddenly what had seemed a benign synchronicity had turned into a trap. But what sort of a trap, that was the question. "Emily," I wanted to yell out, "I know how you felt when you learned that the cigar-smoking bystanders stationed around your house were not a commonplace, but the omens of a larger, possibly more profound, plan."

But instead I remained silent.

I closed my eyes and for a moment the image of the carpet remained on my retina. I squeezed my lids tighter, and held my breath, too, until swimming slowly beneath me there appeared a carpet of a different sort, the one of tall grass I used to ride through on the back of Dominique, when I was just a boy, the two of us leaving a trail of broken stalks like the cursive hand of some neocreationist First Cause, loops and loops of writing going seemingly nowhere, sentences and paragraphs of apparently aimless doodles of the sort you would find on a pad next to a phone, incomprehensible unless viewed (I mean the grass, not the pad) from the cockpit of a plane, a crop duster ready to swoop down with its load of carcinogenic chemicals. And even then, I wondered, what *was* the message?

How simple my life was back then, I thought. Unwilling to break this reverie, I kept my eyes completely shut, and carefully made my way to the bedroom and my bed, where I groped around for a while until I found the feather pillow and laid my head on top of it. And how heedless I was back then, how heedless we both were, Dominique and I, to ever believe that we could travel forever, taking orders and giving them more or less as equals, that a pony and a boy could go on writing in that grass a sentence that would never come to an end because it would never be read, a sentence where each clause would lead, not to a period, but a comma or a semicolon, another clause, and then another, and another, where adjectives could rain down like a stain of fat, cool, wet, heavy, transparent drops that would find themselves spilling not onto the grass that had been their original destination, but onto Dominique's long, attractive nose and my own small sunburnt one, until they reached the ground and collected to form a novel in rivulets, the scratchy graphology of yet another creator (or possibly the same, but miraculously disguised) flowing into streams and rivers, and finally, the library of the ocean herself, to which we are given our library cards at birth, until in the end we have our borrowing privileges revoked once and for all. "How do you like *that* philosophy, Emily?" I thought. Then I began to get a headache, and so with my eyes still shut, I pulled the afghan up beneath my chin and went to sleep.

The next morning I rose, warm and slightly sweaty from my bed. The sun had been out for hours, and clearly it was time for me to do something, to take some kind of action. But what could I do? I walked to my dresser and looked at my socks, which I kept in the top drawer. There they lay, in a variety of colors, none of them in pairs, with several, as nearly as I could tell, missing their partners. (And oh Emily, where were you!) I arranged them all on the clean carpet and put them together, tucking the tops of those that matched into one another. It was a tricky business, because sometimes even when the colors matched, the weave or the pattern did not. A person had to remain alert, I learned. When I finished, I picked up the matched sets and put them back in the drawer. In the end, to my gratification, only two were without a match, although three of the matched pairs had holes, so needed to be discarded.

Emboldened by my success, I opened the next drawer down, the one with my underwear. They too had not been put away properly, so I emptied the drawer's contents, and, separating the t-shirts from the shorts, folded the shirts and rolled the underwear before putting them back, the shorts on the right side and the t-shirts on the left. Then I went to the closet and picked up my regular shirts from the floor and put them on hangers and straightened my ties. I had three ties: one solid, one striped, and one knit. If Emily ever saw my house, I wanted it to be neat.

After finishing all this I was hungry, so I opened the vegetable compartment of the refrigerator, but there were only three carrots, an egg, and a piece of cheese. Leo must have eaten more than I'd noticed at the time. I settled for a couple pieces of whole-wheat toast, and a carrot omelet, then I did the dishes. Finding myself in a dishwashing state of mind, I looked around for other things I could pop into the suds. For some reason I'd accumulated about a dozen ashtrays, even though I didn't smoke, and they in turn had accumulated a formidable residue of grease over the past months. If Emily had been unable to quit her smoking habit (I hoped she'd conquered it), I wanted her to feel comfortable enough to light up and not have an ashtray slip out of her hand. I took an armful of them over to the sink, washed them and set them off to one side to dry. Three were chipped, so those I tossed into the trash along with the socks.

Still possessed by the cleaning demon, I faced the stack of junk mail and magazines that I hadn't bothered to sort those past weeks while I'd been preoccupied with this organ business. Except for one flyer advertising discount cemetery plots, I threw the rest out. The magazines I sorted and bundled with twine, according to their categories. *People* and *Us* made up one stack, *Sports Afield* and *Sports Illustrated* another, the *Journal of Amateur Anthropology* and the *National Geographic* the last. The first two collections I tossed into the dumpster, but these last I carried out to the curb, hoping that some collector might rescue them and take them home. The feature article of the *National Geographic* that crowned that final stack was about Iceland. I stared, not quite knowing why, at the cover, which showed a volcano erupting in the middle of the night. Then I remembered. It was just after Emily and I had made love atop the diving board, when she pulled out a brownish book which she had encased in Saran Wrap to protect it from the steam and heat. The cover was a bright blue, and "Withdrawn" had been stenciled, like a negative personality trait, along the edges of its pages.

"And what might this be?" I'd asked, playfully tugging at the plastic cover. The truth was that I was getting a little tired, and I welcomed the chance just to sit on the board next to Emily as her toes dangled in the water, gently massaging a kidney.

"Stop it," she cried, pulling the book out of my damp hands and cradling it protectively against her flushed, attractive breasts.

"Oh come on," I said. "What is it you're reading that you don't want me to know about?" I was sounding like an ass, I knew, but something had come over me, and I couldn't seem to help it.

"If you must know," she said, "it's a book of Icelandic folk tales. I bought it for a quarter out of the discard rack of my neighborhood library, and just kind of got into them."

Silence on my part. Actually, I was ashamed of the puerile "What is it you're reading" comment, but also, out of nowhere, for some reason the thought of my organ suddenly intruded upon this otherwise pleasant moment. Luckily, it disappeared nearly as quickly as it had arrived.

"Want to read me one?" I asked.

"OK," Emily continued: "Listen: One day, a long, long time ago, Sex and Death were walking down the road. Sex was on one side, and Death was on the other, so you can imagine the scene. On the one side of the road, people were running away as fast as they possibly could to get out of the neighborhood. Animals dove into their burrows, birds veered off, and there was a nearly total silence, because nobody, whether human or animal, wanted to call attention to himself in case Death noticed.

"But on the other side of the road, the Sex one, everybody was waving and jumping up and down like at a rock concert; the birds were knocking into each other overhead, the grouse were copulating on the ground, the wolves were howling, the rabbits were screwing in great fluffy piles. It was everything you might expect — total chaos and excitement."

"Is this really an Icelandic story?" I said. "It sounds incredibly modern. Are you sure you're not just making this up?" I bounced on the diving board a couple of times in a relapse of my boorish habits.

Emily gave me a look. "Well," she said, "It's a modern translation." Then she continued. "And you'd think that Death would have been used to all that by now, but no, for whatever reason, he started to get really depressed, and began to complain. 'They like you; they don't like me; you have all the fun; all I get . . .' blah, blah, blah. . . .

46

"But then you also have to see the two of them," she said, and handed me the book to look at an illustration. It was modern, probably from the seventies, because Sex was in tight-fitting, shiny pants and a shirt split to the navel. Sex wore tons of makeup, had really nice hair, an absolutely dazzling smile, great legs, and was covered with lots of flowers. A guy? A girl? It was hard to tell; in any case, a hippie. And next to Sex was Death, dressed in dark charcoal clothing of course, all torn and muddy, wearing a cloak that concealed who-knew-what? This cloak was made out of the partially cured skins of dozens and dozens of dead (naturally) animals, some as small as mice, others large and heavy. Also, Death was wearing a belt with bunches of dark skulls dangling from it, and Death's own teeth were black and ragged like a speed freak's. Plus, instead of flowers, Death was covered in lots and lots of fungi, mushrooms naturally. Death's hair stuck out in greasy bunches like a biker's.

"Nice pictures," I said.

Emily took the book back. "So then Sex said to Death — and I mean he was genuinely sorry, too — 'Well, you can't blame them, can you? Who would *you* choose if *you* saw the two of us coming down the road?'

"And then Death thought a while, and was very quiet, as if this was the first time in his whole existence he'd ever thought about his appearance and how that affected other people. Not only that, but then he started to feel bad for having been so stupid in addition to everything else. He felt terrible for having frightened so many people and other living things the way he had, because of course nobody, Death included, was ever born wanting to be Death. He just had no choice.

"But then, surprisingly, I must say, Sex, far from being

the sort of self-centered, narcissistic individual most of us have encountered in our own lives, often in the legal profession, turned out to have a real altruistic streak, like a nurse or a minister. Also, truth be told, to be *clamored* at twenty-four hours a day is no picnic either, and who wouldn't like a little peace and quiet once in a while?

" 'OK,' Sex said. 'Here's what I'll do. You put on my clothes, and I'll put on yours, and we see what happens.'

"So they went off behind a bush and Sex gave Death the shirt split to the waist, and applied to Death's very thin lips a really attractive shade of lipstick — possibly the only one in the world that could compliment basically a greenish skin — and added lots of blush, and squirted on some perfume, and even strapped onto Death's long and horny feet these shoes which Sex had kept aside for special occasions, ones with really high heels and covered with red satin.

"In return, Death gave Sex the belt with all those skulls attached by pieces of sinew or something even worse, as well as a serious book of poems that Death saved for coffee shops, the kind of literature that was supposed to convince a person sitting next to him that he wasn't just another creep, but a real intellectual. Also, Death gave Sex a pair of those sunglasses worn by police — the kind where you can't see the eyes at all, but only yourself looking small and distorted.

"Oh, and last of all — Sex also gave Death a light blue baseball cap so completely unthreatening, especially when worn backwards (he told Death to wear it that way), that anyone who saw it could easily begin to imagine eternity as basically your laid-back and totally harmless place, with easy-listening music piped in at all times.

"And so, from that day on to the present, the two have continued to walk along together, Sex on the one side of the road and Death on the other, and ever since then, the two have gotten a far more varied combination of reactions from all whom they meet. These days, as you might guess, Death is a lot happier, and so is Sex."

"My God!" I said. "You found all that in the discard rack of the local library?"

"Yes," said Emily. "You should check it out sometime."

Emily's nipples were small and shy, reminding me for some reason of two prairie dogs on lookout for the rest of the colony.

I felt a familiar stirring in my groin.

Time passed. I did the exercises Dr. Pearlman had suggested, ate lots of cabbage, watched the stain, returned the typewriter to the lady next door who was happy to have it back, and took long walks. I spent a few nights waiting up for the guys on the corner to return but they didn't. I looked through my old catalogues. And threw them out. Then at long last, after about two weeks, Emily returned from her trip. Or more exactly, one afternoon I had left the house to go to the store to buy some fruit juice and some more cabbage, and when I returned there was a message on my answering machine. "Hi, this is Emily. Remember me? Well, I'm back, and we should get together again some time soon, if you're still interested." She left her phone number just in case I'd forgotten it. I played the message several times because I was pretty sure that I could make out some music playing in the background, and not just any music, but "Get Out A My Face," by the Mites, the lyrics of which went:

Hey man, you think you know so much,

Well get out a my face

Cause you ain't so much yourself

Get out a my face,

Get out a my face,

Etc.

I had known the song, and frankly found it scary, doubly so because, in the way the first song any couple hears together automatically becomes "their song," I worried that if "Get Out A My Face" was to be "ours," then what did that portend for our relationship? Or did the fact we had not actually heard it simultaneously, but her first and me later (though I supposed that technically it could be argued that she was listening to it the second time as well), did that mean we still had another chance for something more neutral, like "The Days of Wine and Roses" or "Climb Every Mountain"? And if so, would we ever progress to something more sophisticated, like the movement of a string quartet or an organ (excuse me) solo?

I rushed to the phone, but her line was busy. Then, as I'd just finished making myself a raw cabbage and tuna sandwich for lunch, there was a knock at the door. "Emily," I said, but opened it to find Leo, standing there with a peculiar grin, and holding out a bottle of white liquid with a blue label bordered in lightning bolts. Curiously, I noted that Leo was wearing a plaid sports jacket and a dark tie, not at all his usual costume. When I asked him about it, he replied, "I just happened to be in the neighborhood to attend a memorial service, and your stuff arrived. I thought I'd stop by. If you've got a minute, we'll see how it works."

I noticed that, despite his grin, Leo's face was puffy and

his eyes were a dark pink. I asked him if he wanted a cup of coffee. "I'd like that," he said, and went toward the living room to work while I headed into the kitchen.

In a few minutes Leo returned, smelling strongly of chemicals. "I put some stuff on the spot," he said. "It almost looks as if it's getting worse, but let's wait a few minutes, and we'll see what happens."

"A good idea," I said, and poured Leo some coffee. To go with it I cut some day-old cherry Danish, which I reheated in the microwave.

Then the two of us sat there quietly: me wondering how soon I would see Emily after all the days she had spent away from me, and whether or not I would resent her for everything she had put me through when I finally saw her again. Leo, I supposed, was wondering what was happening to the stain in the next room. Then all at once I saw that I must have been wrong about Leo, because he was crying, his two big shoulders heaving in violent shaking sobs.

I waited a couple minutes for him to settle down before I spoke. "You say you just returned from a memorial service. I hope it wasn't anyone too close."

And that's all it took. The avalanche burst, or I guess re-burst, and Leo lay his head down on the table, some of the cherry filling of the Danish pressing into the wrinkled skin of his forehead. I'd wanted to warn him, but there wasn't time. I got up, picked up my dishes, and carried them to the sink where I stuck them in the water. "You take your time," I said. "If you want to talk about it when you've finished, I'll be happy to listen."

So I washed and dried and put away the dishes, then I walked on over to the television, turned it on and twisted a few knobs. Maybe if Leo came out to see what was going on, he would ask me if anything was wrong with the picture.

"Yes," I would say, "as a matter of fact, there is," but Leo stayed right where he was, sobbing. Finally I gave up, shut it off, and returned to the kitchen, where Leo had for the most part quieted down. He sat up straight, looking hard out the window, the cherry jelly studding the top of one eyebrow like a piece of punk jewelry.

"Is there anything I can do?" I said.

"I think I'm ready now," Leo said. "I know this is a lot to lay on you, but I don't really know anyone else in this town. The fact is that I came here from Milwaukee only a few months ago, and the extraordinary low-cost of the carpet cleaning special you were wise enough to take advantage of was just a part of my overall strategy to establish a broad customer base." A guilty look passed between him and his sadness. "Speaking candidly, I'm obliged to admit from there I planned to gradually start raising the prices. But you've been so nice and all, I just feel ashamed."

I handed him a napkin and pointed to his eyebrow, making the kind of gesture to show him he should wipe in that area. Somehow, words suddenly seemed inadequate. Leo wiped his forehead, getting most of it off, and then looked thoughtfully down at the napkin.

"Yes," he sighed, "it was just a few months ago that Valerie and I moved here to St. Nils. Valerie told me that she wanted to make a new start and to leave her past convictions for kleptomania and passing bad checks behind, so I agreed. We packed everything we owned into that same truck that's parked outside, and left. It was Valerie you spoke to that first time on the phone," Leo added. "But now she's gone."

I must have looked confused, because Leo stopped and fixed me with a look of surprising intensity. "You heard me right," he said. "The memorial service I just attended, with me and the guy from the liquor store down the street as the only mourners, was for Valerie, my wife of twenty-five years. Now, to make matters worse, I find out that the only person I can talk about it with is a distracted (no offense meant), near-total stranger who can't stop fooling with his television."

I explained to Leo that I was sorry not to have known him longer, and assured him that if he remained in St. Nils, I was so happy with the cleaning job he had nearly completed that I would have him do all such work I needed in the future, even if his prices went up just a little. "Especially," I added, "if you've been successful in removing that vexatious stain in the next room."

It didn't seem to help.

"I'm sorry not to have known Valerie," I said. "She sounds like a lovely, though troubled person, and I would have enjoyed having the both of you over to dinner, had I known we would be such friends. But Leo," I said, "some times the amount of time you spend together has little to do with a re-lationship. Just the other day I myself met a person. . . ." Leo wasn't listening.

Instead he took out what appeared to be the same hand-kerchief from the other day, and blew his nose. "What do you say we go check on that stain now?"

"Good," I said. "That's an excellent idea."

And so we brushed the crumbs off our laps (I'd done this earlier for myself when I got up to do the dishes, but then had wound up finishing off a whole other piece of Danish during

Leo's recitation), and we walked together to the living room. To my surprise, the actual stain had completely disappeared, but now the entire section of carpet it had originally covered was an icy white.

"Wow, that stuff was a little stronger than I thought," Leo apologized, "but notice how even the color is. It means that in a couple weeks, when the stain-removing chemicals have neutralized themselves, I can come back and dye the spot back to match the rest of your rug. I promise you'll hardly know the difference. In the meantime, if it bothers you, why don't you take a piece of furniture and put it on top of it. That television, for example, might be a good one to use. . . ."

"And speaking of television," I started to say, when Leo interrupted me again. He had the look that people have in movies when they have something important to say, instead of just blurting it out, as happens in real life.

"Wait a minute," Leo said. "Stop right there. It's true, Paul, that since arriving here in St. Nils I haven't actually gone out to meet many people because Valerie and I kept pretty much to ourselves, but out of everyone I've met here, once I eliminate those late-night phone calls, you've been a real friend." Leo seemed visibly moved. "I have an idea, if you're not offended by my offer. Just before she died, in order to celebrate our twenty-fifth wedding anniversary I bought Valerie and myself an all-expense-paid, nonrefundable trip to Iceland. It was a place she'd always asked me to take her, and if there is such a thing, I guess you could say Valerie was an Icelandophile."

I could see that Leo was starting to relax. All this talking seemed to be helping him.

"I hope you'll excuse my presumption," he said, "but every

54

time I come around here I notice you're not doing much of anything — plus, your color's not so great, either. So just now I thought: maybe a trip would do Paul good. Anyway, here's my offer: if you don't have anything to do right now I would like you to take her place. You seem like a congenial person, and if I go alone, it will only make me sad to know what Valerie is missing. If you want to go, Paul, we leave tomorrow." Then he took a step back, as if to give me time to think.

It was odd, in a way, but out of all the places in the world, I had always wanted to see Iceland, and coincidentally, Dr. Pearlman would be out of town himself for the next few weeks, attending one of those organ conferences/golfing trips in Bermuda he would write off on next year's taxes. And while it was certainly true that I had planned to call Emily as soon as Leo left, and to arrange a meeting, she *had* made me wait for two weeks while she attended to her own business. Besides, I thought it was possible that I was moving too fast, and maybe this dying business was somehow throwing off my sense of proportion. If any relationship was to work, it was important that it be on an equal footing.

"How long is the trip for?" I asked.

"Just a week," Leo said.

"Can you wait a minute?" I said, "I need to check something."

I walked over to the phone and dialed Emily's number. Sure enough, it was still busy.

"Thanks," I replied, "I'll go."

55

III

The airport at Reykjavik was pretty much what anyone would imagine, even someone like me, who hadn't ever been to Iceland. It was drafty, with snack bars serving varieties of fish and hot tea, large ceramic tiles glazed with hopelessly cheery colors, bullet-shaped dark receptacles for trash, and blond depressed characters hanging around a place that seemed to embody what once must have been a comforting idea of motion, even if only just for others. Still, the total effect was that despite the dark, the cold, and the late hour, there seemed to be actually something strangely festive about the place. It was as if for those hapless human beings still stuck to this island-sized block of ice, any motion at all, even vicarious, even the arrivals and departures of total strangers, was in itself a cause for celebration. I studied Leo to see if any of the semi-joyful ambiance of the place had taken hold, but it had not, and even at the very start of the flight, he seemed to have sunken into a moraine of introspection too deep for me to pull him out.

At first, I had explained Leo's silence as medically related.

"I've got this asthma," Leo had told me. "It's important for me to stay as calm as possible."

So it was that during the takeoff I watched as Leo wheezed prayers beneath his breath, his eyes shut tight, his big hands gripping the armrests of his seat, and waited for him to relax. But after that things didn't improve, and for the rest of the flight Leo generally sat staring out the blank window to my left. Occasionally he would sigh, or mumble "clouds," or "bird," but for the most part, all his happy repartee about cleaning carpets seemed to have been swept away. I attempted to cheer him up with interesting conversation, but was rebuffed.

"Leo," I said, "what are you most looking forward to seeing on our visit to Iceland?"

Silence. My swimmer's ear had cleared up.

In truth, the only real conversation we had at all was when, following our in-flight meal (a surprisingly light and delicate herring soufflé, a fresh green salad, French bread, coffee and plum tart), Leo rose slightly and reached into his wallet to extract the one picture he had brought with him of his late wife. It had been taken, he said, on their honeymoon in Bermuda, and in a way, I supposed that Leo was showing Valerie the plane at the same time he was showing me Valerie. In the photo she was leaning rather dangerously against a gray sea wall, and held in the crook of one arm a large straw purse stuffed with three or four towels bearing the partially obscured name of a hotel, the Bel-something-or-other. Valerie had been a small, dark-haired woman, and looked fresh and happy, as if she really believed this was the beginning of a wonderful journey, one that would move unceasingly from triumph to triumph, culminating, I suppose, in a bouquet of adoring grandchildren. She appeared to be about nineteen.

"Those were the happiest days of my life," Leo told me. "Back then Valerie was just swiping linen and the odd piece of flatware. In those days when her checks bounced it was only because she hadn't paid attention to her bank balance. Not only that, but she was crazy about me. I remember once when we were first married, the evening news had a story that some fourth grader had pulled out a rifle and shot six or seven of his classmates. That night Valerie actually slept curled in a quilt outside the front door of our apartment because she said she didn't want me getting hurt. And the next day she wouldn't let me out, or the day after that, or after that, until a week had passed and there wasn't much to eat but her homemade pasta, which she fried up in a little butter. Then finally we ran out of that, too. I lost my job because of it, but that's how much that woman loved me. And now, I'm flying to Iceland with practically a total stranger instead of her. Imagine."

Leo slumped down. His eyes were stuck on the crossword of the in-flight magazine. "Do you know a seven letter word that means transitory?" he asked, and I was just about to answer, when he put his head to his chest and fell asleep.

Standing in the drafty airport terminal, waiting for our luggage, I checked my watch, and all at once it was my own turn to lose myself in the surprisingly sticky webs of my own memory. The motion of my watch, first out of the corner of an eye, and then staring directly at it, made me remember how Emily had kept her watch, waterproof, of course, secured to her wrist throughout all the passionate nakedness of our encounter. It was heavy and black, attached by a black plastic strap, and waterproof to one hundred meters. Emily said that she found it difficult to be without.

At that exact moment, I recalled, we both were gently dog paddling past a set of lungs basking on the surface, and trying our best not to bump a small, persistent thyroid. "This may sound ridiculous," Emily had said, panting slightly, "but I wear this watch to project a hypothetical net of forward motion over a future which, without a timepiece of some sort, would be only a blank and spacious wasteland: the dial of a clockface without either hands or numbers.

"It may seem silly," she continued, steering around a testicle which somehow had got out of the kiddy pool, "but if I can anticipate the steady, regular progress of the big hand, say over the next fifteen minutes, then I can anticipate as well the motion of my own body (and yours, too) over that exact period of time. Not predict, mind you, but merely anticipate, and though there are well-known groups whose slogan is 'One day at a time,' I find it more appropriate to keep it to fifteen or twenty minutes, unless, of course, you're able to make it last longer." She took a wet strand of her hair and swam for a while with it between her lips. She must have a thing for hair, I remember thinking.

"Not that this was always the case," Emily added. "There was a time, years ago, when I was so perfectly attuned to the rhythms of the universe that I never needed to wear a watch at all. You would ask me the time, and I would say, 'Five twenty-seven.' You could say, 'Meet me two hours from now on the corner of such and such; and at exactly two hours from that time I'd be there. You could say, 'Two months from now in a certain city, I'd like to meet for a light lunch in a pleasant café I know about with outdoor tables and real cloth napkins,' and I'd be there five minutes early because I don't like to keep people waiting. By the way, during those days my periods also came like clockwork."

Emily seemed to be directing her thoughts toward an area I couldn't comprehend at the moment, so I swam closer, to indicate my attention.

"But little by little, I began running slow. Instead of five minutes early, I'd be on time, and then five minutes late, and ten, and twenty. I tried to speed up, but then I lost all sense of time completely, so finally, I became like all people. I went out and bought a watch, and my faith in a future returned. Now here you are." We were at the shallow end. She pulled herself out and kissed me, leaving me to wonder what all that time business had been about, anyway.

At last our luggage arrived. I retrieved it and carried it back to Leo, whom I had left alone on a plastic bench. Whatever process Leo had begun on the plane had gotten worse, and his sighs had gradually turned to long introspective silences, with an occasional short sob. Leo's breakdown at my kitchen table, I speculated, far from being an exception may well have been the rule. Not surprisingly, in this state of mind, Leo had also neglected to make reservations at any hotel. I left him guarding our luggage in his fashion, and made my way across the concourse to a shabby booth set beneath an off-white vinyl banner that read "Hotels & Volcano Tours."

Although it took the tour representative, who only moments earlier had been dozing with a stack of brochures for a pillow, a beat or two to chase the cobwebs from his mind, once in action he turned out to be exceedingly helpful. Not only could he recommend an excellent, inexpensive hotel, he said, but when I asked him for an activity that might cheer up my friend, he booked us on a discount volcano tour with one of their best guides. "A volcano. Lava. Fire. Ice. Who can be sad?" he said. "Plus this guide, she speaks perfect English, and is not very hard on the eyes, either." Then, after accepting a deposit for a tour the following day, he excused himself to go to the restroom where, he said, he would wash up a bit to remove some of the ink from the brochures which seemed to have adhered to his face.

The hotel proved to be everything that the man at the booth had promised. It was clean and comfortable, with heated, firm mattresses, and out of deference to Leo's generosity, I gave him his first choice of beds. We both slept wonderfully. The next morning the rest appeared to have cheered Leo up enough to elicit a variety of appreciative and scornful comments about the carpets in the place. We enjoyed a breakfast of fried potatoes, cod, and fresh coffee that was brought to our rooms. Then, being sure to dress warmly, we made our way down to the lobby to meet our guide, Greta.

Greta, it turned out, was about the same age as Emily — her early thirties, I guessed — but she was fair where Emily had been suntanned, almost as if a photograph of Emily had been taken by some itinerant photographer who had forgotten to print it, and left behind only the negative. Greta shared the blond, almost transparent hair of many of her countrymen, was tall (a little taller than Emily) and slender (about Emily's weight), with straight, thick eyebrows (the same as Emily's). Her legs, however, were thin, almost too much so, and her feet were wrapped in smooth, dark, fur-covered boots.

"They're baby seal," Greta told me when she noticed me staring at them. "Back in the days I bought them I was a girl of seventeen or eighteen, and was unaware that to obtain such fur, men first had to walk out onto the red-stained ice, carrying heavy clubs and baseball bats, and club the pups, as they are called, to death. Not only that, but did you know that many of these adorable creatures are not killed outright, but survive for hours, and sometimes days in an agony incomprehensible to human beings, until at last many of them — and surely it must come as an ironic mercy — find themselves being skinned alive. When I learned all this, however, the boots had long been paid for." Then she blushed.

I was surprised at the honesty of her revelation. Were all Icelanders so forthright and so practical?

Greta said that she had been the lead singer in a rock band, The Snowmen, for quite a while, and to right this injustice she had already written at least a dozen songs about the plight of these helpless animals. The result was a near-complete boycott of the band by their local audience who had, she sniffed, somehow confused the clubbing to death of baby seals with their manhood. "Iceland is a small place," she continued, "and partly as a result of this ostracism I began taking drugs to ease the pain. Then it got out of hand, and I did a stint in rehab. The band is still together, though barely, and to make ends meet, I took the job as a guide with Volcano Tours.

"I haven't been with them all that long," she said, "but one of the benefits is the chance to meet fascinating people, like yourselves."

Then we walked outside where we all piled into her snow tire-shod Volkswagen Rabbit, and began the drive to our destination. "Even though this is the only working volcano that's within easy reach of the general public," Greta laughed, emitting a pleasant, salty breath, "it's surprising how few people actually go there."

To begin with, the place was strangely deserted.

To follow that, there was heat, redness, more heat, and even more redness. Acrid choking gasses and soot. More soot. Still more soot. The air full of dark, eye-smarting particles.

"Here, put on these goggles. We give them to everyone who gets this far," Greta said, and passed out two pairs of old, scratched skiing goggles.

"You mean," I said, "some people actually change their minds and head back?" but my voice was buried beneath the crunch of boot soles and heels on the still-warm cinders that coated the narrow path spiraling down to the earth's hot core. The roar of combustion. The rush of air. Leo wheezing as Greta and I trudged onward. I knew it was probably just the asthma, but still I was oddly pleased to see that, even with my organ the way it was, I was in less bad shape than Leo. Then Leo bent over, his knuckles white as they clutched the birch staff Greta had pulled from the surprisingly roomy trunk of the Volkswagen and handed him at the beginning of our tour ("Here, why don't you take this along just in case one of us needs it?" Tactful, I had noted). Scattered bits of conversation, and deep, rasping coughs, impeded by the rush of air up from the center cone of the volcano:

"Wow! Will you guys take a look down there!"

"Say, did I ever tell you about my fear of heights?" Cough, cough. "Now that I think of it, maybe that's why I became a rug cleaner."

"Do you want to turn back?"

"No (cough), I'll be fine. How's your organ?" I had told Leo about my organ in an effort to cheer him up a little on the flight over.

And then it arrived at last: terror. The real, deep-down primal stuff. The loins of all creation. A trio of faces, two guys and a girl, and not in some boardroom of a major corporation, under cool, fluorescent lights and with yellow pads that a secretary has handed around to take notes on, but lit by a hellish glow. We wiped the lenses of our goggles to keep them clean, and the soot smudged beneath our fingers like typewriter ink. Molecules of our sweat no sooner made their blind exits from assorted pores than they were swept up into the air, like Popsicle sticks tossed into a flood-engorged river. We pressed beautiful, handmade handkerchiefs (also passed out by Greta at the beginning of the tour) to our noses to prevent the hair inside them from being singed. Amazingly, throughout it all, behind the smudgy lenses of her shatterproof goggles, Greta's eyes, large and calm, still remained their attractive shade of grayish violet.

Then: "You know, I have a confession to make. This is actually my first time as a tour guide, so there's a small possibility I got the wrong volcano. Do you want to turn back and try another?"

Gentlemanly protestations, and renewed resolve to continue.

Greta's sweat-soaked, soot-covered jumpsuit revealed the curves of her body in unexpected ways: pale crescents where the soot had been unable to cling. Shadows were cast above our heads into the particle-laden air, and three distorted shapes writhed in the reddish smoke, like three souls in a special-effect-heavy version of *The Inferno*. Suddenly another surprise:

the crunch of potato chips as Greta opened a pack and passed it around.

"Here, the salt might do you good. And here's some water."

Cough, cough.

"Thanks. That hit the spot."

A smear of cinders across Greta's forehead gave her the look of a Caribbean pirate queen. Very becoming, I thought, despite myself.

"I don't feel (cough) so good."

"Oh, come on, Leo. It's just a little farther" — that one from me.

More hurt. Still thicker smoke. Harder yet to breathe. A volley of accusations, followed by reassurances:

"Whose idea was it to come here anyway?"

"Don't worry. We can turn back if you like, but we're almost there."

"No, I can do it." Cough.

Then a few steps more. The hiss of steam. A whoosh. A glacier dissolved before our wondering eyes. What a sight! Coming right out of the side of the volcano itself: fire, and a wall of ice. Then air, all swirling. The result: beneath our narrow path, an underground river rushed downward straight into the heart of the flames. All the ancient elements of classical Greece in contention: Know thyself. The Golden Mean. Zeus and Hera. Apollo and Dionysis. *The Iliad. The Odyssey.*

"Wasn't this worth the trip?"

"Do you (cough) mind (cough) terribly if (cough) we stop and rest a while?"

And so, we three tired pilgrims rested for a moment. Greta and I took healthy swallows from our respective water bottles, now nearly empty, while Leo sat, his eyes glazed by the heat, panting in low, shallow breaths, his skin turning gray. I noticed that at one time or another Greta must have torn a hole in one of the thighs of her toreador-fitting jumpsuit, and a sooty piece of skin peeked out.

Looking over the ledge, I was suddenly reminded of a story that Emily had told me regarding the subject of fire. Back when I heard it (ironically, it seemed at that moment) I was surrounded by water, lying on my stomach, sharing a gigantic plastic pool float with Emily. I was admiring Emily's smooth and girlish heels, the tender skin behind her knees, the oh-so-unbelievably soft skin of her pale inner thighs, the sly curve of her buttocks, the tender depression of her lower back through the center of which ran, like a buried telephone cable, her spine, and of course her shoulder blades. Actually my neck was starting to hurt from having to lift my head to see all this, when I casually noticed a reddened patch of skin the size of a quarter on one of her shoulders.

"You're starting to burn," I said. "Would you like me to rub on a little sunscreen?"

Emily laughed. "Sunscreen is one of the things absolutely forbidden here. It's harmful to the organs. Anyway, that spot isn't a sunburn but an old scar."

"A scar," I said, and she explained.

At one point in her childhood, she said, being curious to explore the world around her, she had reached up to the top of her mother's stove and pulled down on her face and back a pot of boiling water in which her mother was sterilizing a set of Tupperware. Though the hot, plastic, useful serving containers hurt as they crashed into her, Emily said, they were nothing

66

compared to the boiling water. "Nevertheless," she told me, "I learned something from the event: as I walked down the road with my mother, Lonnie, to make the long trek to the emergency room from our farm, I was struck for the first time by the fact that while the damage done by air or earth goes away immediately after the offending element disappears, the place where fire has been continues to burn long after the flame has been removed."

Then Emily rolled toward me, and our plastic float rocked dangerously in the pool. "It's as if," she said, ignoring the instability of our platform, "the memory of fire is stored, not in our minds, as are the other elements, but in the very tissues of our bodies themselves."

I gripped the sides of the float as tightly as I could and tried to keep from slipping off.

Emily continued. "Fire must be the most primal memory of all, that of the cosmic explosion which began the universe itself: the memory of memory."

Then the float grew steady again, and at last, when it bumped into the side of the pool, Emily got off and walked over to a coil of hose still attached to a spigot. As if she were burning up through her very memory of the subject, she turned it on and let the cool water run from her head to her feet. Then she shut it off and sat back down.

"You know," she explained, "it's no surprise that followers of the Buddhist religion often refer to the human body as 'a burning house.' For that matter, how many times when you were a child did you advise a ladybug to 'fly away home.' Or, to be even more explicit, how many times did you also tell her, 'Your house is on fire and your children are burning.' So if the house, in this case, is the human body, and the children are those things of the flesh we long for, as in the phrase 'burning with desire,' then 'home' must mean the dwelling of our spirit, for though we can have many houses, there is always only one true home."

Still balanced on the float, which was slimy from whatever stuff they filled the pool with, I felt dizzy. I could scarcely believe that this naked woman, a stranger only hours earlier, had been able to create such a rich web of metaphor in addition to her earlier penchant for philosophical inquiry.

Emily touched her red spot thoughtfully. She reached out a hand to help me ashore, and then, as if she was suddenly self-conscious of the display of further erudition that was about to follow, blushed. "I once took a course in Zoology of the Spirit," she said, "that pointed out that the Ladybug herself is half feminine (the lady part) and half impersonal (the bug part) in the exact way that insects themselves seem to mirror the workings of the universe. And just as in Whitman's famous poem, 'A Noiseless Patient Spider,' where the spider is identified with the soul, so in the child's verse just quoted, the Ladybug herself *is* the soul, or anima, which has left her home, by which I mean, of course, eternity."

Amazed at what I had just heard, I let her kiss me full on my lips again. Then we moved to a heap of old water polo net that lay in a corner and we made love. It was surprisingly comfortable.

Phew. I assumed the fumes had been getting to me, because suddenly I was reeled back into the difficult present by Greta's not-so gentle grip on my arm. She pulled me closer to half-yell into my ear above the rush of air. "It doesn't look like

Leo's getting any better. Maybe we should walk him over to that little rocky shelf over there. The two of us can go on down, and then we can return for Leo on the way back."

I studied Leo. His eyes were now protruding in a most uncomfortable-looking manner, and the glaze on his goggles had darkened to a brownish film. His skin, formerly only gray, had gone to being mottled with patches of red, white and blue. "That's a good idea," I said. "I'll ask him if he minds."

Together, Greta and I gently slapped Leo a few times to bring him out of his stupor. Then, dragging him to his feet, we half-walked, half-pulled Leo downward toward the safety of the shelf. His legs seemed simultaneously stiff and rubbery, if that was possible. The heat grew in intensity, as did the thickness of the smoke that filled, or rather substituted for the air we were trying to breath. Whatever it was, it was a greenish, yellowish, brownish color, and I remember thinking there was no way it could be healthy. How was it possible for poor Leo to breathe in these conditions, I worried, when even my own lungs had seriously begun to ache? I signaled Greta to stop for a moment. Then, letting Greta support most of Leo's saggy weight, I stepped back to take a look at the exhausted rug cleaner. Weirdly, Leo seemed to be better in a way, although it was impossible to see if his eyes were open or shut, covered as the goggles were with soot.

"Leo," I said, "would you like to wait here for a few minutes till we get back?"

Leo stood for a moment, wobbled, and let out a fairly negative-sounding moan.

"Leo," I repeated, "are you sure you want to go on with this right to the end?"

This time Leo's moan sounded much more positive. The exercise must have helped, I hoped.

"Do you think that we can do it?" I asked Greta.

"We're almost there, I think," Greta said as the smoke closed in around us. "Let's give it a try."

At last, finally, eventually, simultaneously, ultimately, opportunely, this party of three reached our goal: a narrow ledge from which it was possible to stare down through a space where the smoke was momentarily diverted by a surprising current of fresh air, and to breathe half clearly for a minute. There we peered a thousand feet down into the molten glow of the burning rock itself as if it was a fierce, hot eye, and we, the three of us, tiny and dust mote-sized, the objects of its scrutiny. The effect, combined with the sudden presence of the breathable air, was hypnotic.

How long we stood there, shifting from one foot to the other, staring into that bright light which became, in my own, if not everyone's fevered imagination, the very womb of the earth itself, I can't say. Then the ground shifted, or seemed to, because I was unable to be sure of where I was, or even who. But whoever I was, I looked over at Greta to see whether she was alarmed as well, or was this just a normal sort of event that took place often here in Iceland. After all, I was just a visitor there, I thought, and as those very words passed through my head I heard a tiny scrape of gravel. Greta's face assumed a horrified expression, and I whirled around to see Leo wobbling on the lip of the ledge. Without hesitating, I reached out to pull Leo back, but possibly in my panic I did so a bit too forcefully, for even that well-meaning motion appeared to be all it took to destroy the little sense of balance Leo had at his command.

There was a "whoops!" and then only an empty space where Leo had been.

What really happened, even to this day I cannot say with absolute certainty. It was possible, I decided (much later) that having been unconscious, Leo had been awakened too suddenly, and the result was that he toppled forward, or just plain slipped. It was even conceivable that in a sudden fit of longing for the dead Valerie (I couldn't be sure how personal that womb-of-the-earth vision was), Leo had willingly followed Valerie to the grave, and, like one of those Japanese love suicides, but with a time delay of several weeks, had leapt willingly to his own death.

I stared after Leo's feeble arc in the glowing darkness, watching until I believed I could see a tiny flare of something explode down at the very bottom of the pit. "Good-bye," I shouted down into the abyss, "and good luck, my friend."

And then, unbidden, Emily's exact words as she described her one in-home accident with boiling water floated back to me. "I could see the pot," she had said, "and the fire, and even myself, as if the three of us were a story to be explored, a trium-virate of relationships so basic, yet enigmatic, that the only way I could understand them was to reach up, take hold of that handle, and pull it toward me."

The ground of the volcano shook again in an up, down, and sideways motion. I looked away from the fiery pit, and could tell from Greta's terrified expression that this was no ordinary occurrence. "Hurry," she said, taking my hand with her long and slender fingers, "Let's get out of here."

But as luck would have it, the very force of her gesture, in a horrible replay of my own earlier Helping Hand toward Leo, had precisely the same result. Namely, the two of us were momentarily knocked off balance, toppled together over the edge like the two fat clay wings of a butterfly made by some third grader in art class, heavy and falling downward toward the oven where the butterfly would be baked, cooled, painted, and finally, I supposed, lain flat on a shelf along with thirty like it in preparation for Parents' Night.

Such were my thoughts, and if things had gone as I had guessed, their banality would have remained forever buried beneath a mound of ash and fire. Yet, as even I could plainly see, I was still there. I remained alive, and the reason was amazingly simple: Unlike Leo, who appeared to have entered the very eye (or whatever) of the burning core of the volcano with the clean swish of a basketball passing through a hoop, the eccentric shape formed by Greta and I must have caused us first to careen, then bounce, then roll hand in hand down the sides of the crater itself, its hot jagged cinders ripping off our clothing and abrading our skin, dropping us with dizzying speed, like (to use yet another simile) a horribly deformed ball down a funnel-shaped roulette wheel of the sort that only appears in dream sequences of bad motion pictures (and once in a while in real nightmares too), the sort with only one possible outcome. And yet.

So the two of us bounced and tumbled, and clung to each other as I kept my eyes shut tighter than I ever had for any bedtime reverie, eyes that were already stinging from the soot and debris that had somehow worked their way behind my eyelids, as the air around me grew yet more intensely hot and yet more painful. Still we held on, me to Greta and Greta to me, and plunged together (maybe, it occurred to me, *we* were the two doomed lovers in the Japanese tale I'd pinned to Leo only moments earlier!) straight into the final heartbreaking resolution (or whatever) of our own personal volcano.

Suddenly, in the midst of all these thoughts and emotions (mostly fear, I confess), I felt a spurt of scalding steam. But before I could fully register this new degree of pain and find a spot for it on the informal scale of discomfort that I had, unconsciously, it seemed, been creating — it stopped. I found myself in a stream of water as icily cold as the former steam had been hot. Whatever this new water was, it came with such force as to knock my goggles off and simultaneously rinse out my eyes, so that at least they felt a lot better. I opened them wide to find everything totally dark. Gradually, I realized I must be in the grip of a swift, glacial, underground river that emanated from the volcano itself. It seemed that instead of being baked, I was slated to drown, but before I had the chance to further savor the irony (or maybe just misperception), Greta's hand was swept out of mine. I blinked, once, twice, and a faint light surrounded me. Had I passed through this life to the other side? Well, obviously no, but I didn't know it at the time. Then my head rose above the water; I gulped air, and behind me I heard a similar gulping noise. Quickly, I turned to see the walls of a lava tube shooting by at an alarming rate, and Greta, her head barely above the surface, gulping like crazy, being swept away with me in a sort of natural sluice, down the side of the mountain. Then everything grew dark once again.

And it stayed dark, but the water turned warm. My guess was that it was from the presence of a rivulet of lava, but before I could explore that thought further, I was cold again. Then warm again. Then the current slowed, and finally stopped, and I found myself in a quiet pool.

"Greta," I called out to see if she had accompanied me all the way on this journey or had somehow been diverted, and my voice echoed in the moist air.

To my joy, I heard an answering call: "Behind you. I'm over here."

I paddled to where the voice came from, and after a moment of searching was close enough to hold her. There was finally light to see, and I couldn't help but notice that our double tumble down the inner slope of the volcano and our subsequent dual watery descent had removed Greta's clothes as well as mine. I paddled a few feet away so as not to embarrass her, and was in the midst of reflecting on how lucky we were to be alive when I heard Greta splashing toward me (she wasn't much of a swimmer). Then, in a sort of spontaneous gesture Greta pulled me close, forcing me to tread water for the both of us.

"Hush," she said, although I was not aware of having said anything. So we clung together against the gentle backdrop of the splashing water as it trickled into our pool and echoed against the ceiling of the darkened chamber. As so often happens in life and death situations like this one, I could feel my body, relieved at having been given what for all it could tell was only a momentary reprieve, preparing to replicate itself as quickly as humanly possible.

So we made love, rapidly and often, like those near-mythic lovers at the end of those romantic movies where one of them, usually the woman, is inside the train that's pulling out of the station, and the other, the guy, is running alongside, breathing hard and shouting out the feelings that he's kept hidden those many years, yet which, tragically, she can't hear above the roar of the wheels on the tracks, but then, at the last minute, he gets

74

on board, makes his way to her compartment, and the shades go down.

Or, alternatively, we were like two passengers on a sinking ocean liner, trapped in our tastefully decorated stateroom, while unknown to us, the entire ship was already far beneath the surface of the water, the two of us still alive only because we were trapped inside a gigantic bubble of air. Nevertheless, though completely unaware of the situation, still, in some mysterious way we *must* have known about the danger (possibly from the ringing in our ears due to water pressure), because there we were frantically throwing off all our fancy dress clothes, abandoning all sense of foreplay, or even play, and instead replacing it with one single, gasping, desperate, last, passionate, inchoate, sincere, blind consummation before the oxygen was absolutely gone.

Or possibly we were two astronauts from different nations, of different backgrounds and different cultures, but both fortunately speaking English, who were inside a space station that was hit by a meteorite carrying an alien life-form which, totally unknown to us, had already dissolved our fellow crew members into a pool of bluish motor oil beyond the airlock, and, its appetite scarcely whetted, was about to make its way to the two of us, who were together sleeping in the last remaining compartment, when one of us, probably Greta, woke, and shook me awake to ask, "What's that funny smell?"

"What smell?" I answered groggily (I always did have a hard time waking up), but before I could answer, there was Greta tugging at the zippers of my space suit like a woman possessed, and pulling off my trousers.

In any case, back in the dark, Jacuzzi-like atmosphere of

the underground pool I found myself so relaxed (naturally, it's impossible for me to speak for Greta) that I failed to notice that even as we made grateful, happy love, we were also gently being carried along by the current. Thus it was that the very moment we both screamed our conjoined mutual pleasure, we passed, in a startling visual accompaniment, through the opening of the cavern out into the pale, white light of the Icelandic morn, startling two very sleepy-looking campers.

Above them loomed the enormous pyramid of the volcano, beneath which their tent was pitched on a carpet of snow, pure white, except for an unsightly, yellow stain about twenty yards above it, where a noxious formerly subterranean emission must have been recently deposited.

"You out there — are you all right?" the shorter one shouted in English. He was wearing a visored cap and yellow gloves that gave him an oddly duckish appearance. At that moment I was out of breath, and I guess Greta was too, so we settled for paddling ourselves to the bank where he stood waiting.

"Good morning," he said. "My name is Sonny, and my friend here is Dane. You look to be in some difficulty. If you'll wait for a moment we'll wrap you in the emergency survival blanket made of quilted aluminum on one side to hold in the heat, and black, marked with yellow strips so as to be easily seen from the air, on the other, which I happen to have with me. Actually, it's not at all surprising I have such a blanket, because the laws of Iceland require that each citizen carry one with him or her at all times. By the way, in addition, both Dane and I are professional outdoorsmen, so we take no notice of your nakedness. But even if we did, because of the lack of puritan prudery in our Icelandic culture I want you to know we are receiving far less vicarious pleasure from the sight of you, and especially the attractive lady who is splashing stark naked next to you, than would most of your own countrymen (I say this just in case you are an American, or possibly English; if you are French, of course, you can ignore it). Have no fear; the crime rate here in Iceland is among the lowest in the world, and it is our sincere wish that you and your beautiful lady friend be returned safely to your habitat as soon as possible."

I bobbed in the water a bit. The air was chilly, and the water, heated as it was, wasn't actually too bad.

Sonny walked to his tent, where, after rummaging around for a fairly long time, he emerged carrying two small shiny packages. We crawled out of the river and stood there shivering on the bank. At last, after some initial difficulty with the packaging, he opened one and wrapped it around Greta. The other he tossed to me. It might have been the cold, or the overcast conditions, but the blanket didn't seem to help all that much.

"The two of us usually make our living as guides to rich sportsmen, or maybe I should say 'sportspersons,' " Dane said, nodding to Greta. "As you may know, these wealthy individuals often come to our country in search of salmon, and so we drove up to this stream yesterday, while it's still the off-season, to check on its potential as a destination for our clients. You can imagine our surprise, having risen early this morning, we were just rinsing out our coffee cups and brushing the snow off our parkas, preparing to begin our hike up the eastern slope of the volcano, when the two of you orgasmically exited its very core. But here I am, talking about us. What brings the two of you here?"

Greta said something brief in Icelandic, over which the two men laughed uproariously. Then Sonny went back into the tent and returned with two real, woolen blankets. They helped. The men brewed another pot of coffee, and as I sipped it slowly, I heard Greta telling what I guessed was the story of our trip, for among the incomprehensible native speech that I did not understand, I believed that I heard the word "Leo," repeated several times, and then what sounded like "French fry."

When Greta had finished and I had begun to feel a little better, Dane turned back to me and spoke in nearly perfect English. "Just over the hill is our four-wheel-drive vehicle. If you feel up to it we can all walk there, then the two of us will drive you into town where the lady can call Volcano Tours and tell them where to pick up the car."

Oddly, my first real introduction to Iceland came on that very trip back to town. I soon learned that Icelanders were a gentle and hospitable people, and, according to Dane and Sonny, Icelanders did not have family names, but instead generally used a last name that combined their father's first name and "son" if they were a male, or "dottir" if they were a female. Thus, as is often the case all over the world, if a son were named after his father, in Iceland Sonny's son's name would be Sonny Sonnyson, etcetera. For a moment I had the dizzying sensation of a man standing in front of a mirror looking into a mirror, and so on, forever.

As the four of us drove we watched the sun rise higher. It was turning out to be a beautiful day. The increasingly distant slopes of the volcano were silhouetted against the blue sky, and the river engraved itself like a scalpel into the white flabby flesh of its banks. By way of passing the time, our two helpful guides also told me that although most Icelanders, especially in the larger cities, dressed much the same as the residents of other European countries, on holidays it was not uncommon for some women to wear a traditional black, heat-absorbing dress, with gold threads.

Curiously (and Dane had no explanation for this), Icelanders consumed far more lamb than did people of other countries. Even hot dogs in Iceland were made, rather than of beef or pork or chicken or healthy tofu as in St. Nils, of lamb. "We also enjoy boiled sheep's head," Dane rather shamefacedly admitted. Not to be outdone, Sonny added that their favorite dessert was "skyr" made from curds of milk. Both agreed that the nation's consumption of hard liquor was considerable, bordering on the unhealthy. Then, perhaps uncomfortable with that subject, Dane informed me that Iceland was a republic, though with strong ties to Denmark, hence his own name. The citizens elected a president who served four years, but the Prime Minister, and Cabinet, appointed by the parliament, the Althing, actually directed national policy.

Out of the corner of my eye I caught the blur of something large and white that might have been a polar bear, but before I could ask, Sonny interjected, "And not an easy job it is, what with six main political parties, these being the Independence Party, the Citizen's Party, the Woman's List, The People's Alliance Party, The Progressive Party, and the Social Democratic Party."

Greta laughed. "You two sound like you've been reading the almanac."

"That's exactly what we've been doing," Dane answered. "You can make good money at the Governmental Trivia contests at the Cod Fishers' Rest on Monday nights." I filed away that information, should I ever need it.

During the long winter nights both men reported that they spent much of their time, when not at "The Rest," watching *Jeopardy* and *Wheel of Fortune* on large Japanese televisions. They told me that their houses were warm and snug, constructed from reinforced concrete, and painted, along with those of most of their neighbors', in pleasant pastels. I turned to Greta to see how she was reacting to this conversation, none of which must have been news to her. Exhausted by her ordeal, she dozed next to me in the back seat, her blond head resting lightly on the window.

Suddenly, there was a bump and we had arrived at a large, white hospital. Then someone came up and called Greta away. She made motions, like "stay right there," and so that's exactly what I did.

How had time passed so quickly? One moment I was on the inner shelf of an active volcano with a beautiful guide and an asthmatic rug cleaner, and the next I had arrived in a place that was safe and secure, the gleaming emergency room of a modern hospital. In the heady aftermath of our rescue, for a moment I forgot my former organ troubles. Suddenly I remembered something Emily had said as she dried herself off with an increasingly damp, coarse-textured towel, for the fourth or fifth time that afternoon a couple weeks ago.

On that day I think I'd mentioned something about a theory I'd read about in a magazine in Dr. Pearlman's office. It said that taking large doses of antibiotics prior to the transplant was helpful in reducing post-operative infection. No sooner had I said it when Emily let out a surprisingly vigorous snort. "Antibiotics," she said, "don't even talk to me about antibiotics. Do you remember how I told you that I was raised on a farm?"

I told her I did.

"Well," Emily said, "the reason was, although I didn't know it at the time, that my parents, Brad and Lonnie, had two big problems. And it was the first, their near-fanatical obsession with cleanliness, that led to their second, the fact that they also had a serious antibiotic abuse problem. This, by the way, is not as unusual as it sounds, because agricultural areas are famous for the large amounts of such drugs dispensed to animals on a daily basis, and I now think that must be why they moved there. To this day I can remember how Brad used to say, 'If we can't catch every germ before it enters our bodies, then we'll sure as hell get them once they're stuck inside.'"

Emily shook out her hair and continued. "Of course, like a lot of junkies, they preferred to indulge their habit in the company of others, and I still have nightmares about being in the bedroom of a neighboring farm where I would often fall asleep as a child. The friendly couple who lived there turned out to be, of course, major antibiotic suppliers, and Brad and Lonnie used to leave me resting on their antique, four-poster bed while they quietly got high in the next room on Keflex or Tetracycline.

"In any case, on one of the bedroom's walls (as on the walls of so many rooms in those days, even in the Midwest) there was a bad reproduction of Munch's *Scream*. On the opposite wall was a poster of Mr. Natural that I would stare at for hours in the blue light of a lava lamp while I lay on the stained batik bedspread. Unbearably warm, because the temperature of most of those drug pads was kept deliberately high, I would lie there and pretend I was being kissed by Mr. Natural himself, his uncombed beard tickling me until I fell asleep. And yes, I can still recall the exact sweet smell of the incense burned those nights, a cross between cinnamon, hay, and airplane glue, together with the mind-numbing beat of The Loving Spoonful in the next room, and the scratchy fantasy of Mr. Natural going down on me as I tried to stay awake.

"I don't want you to be offended," Emily explained, "but there's a reason I'm bringing this up. All these flashbacks which I'm experiencing even now make me wonder about the two of us, our future — yours and mine. I mean, at this moment we seem so close, so intimate, as we enjoy a poolside setting both strange (especially for you, I guess) and familiar. But will we meet again? Years from now will I remember you? Or will the memory of this day and us disappear, be slowly absorbed, like so many others, into the stain of that old batik bedspread? When I hear your voice, will it be yours, or only The Spoonful spliced together with Munch's *Scream*? Will I smell the sensual musk of your armpits, as I do at this moment, or will that also have been elbowed out of the olfactory picture by that stupid incense? Will I remember the silken touch of your hard-muscled body, or only the whiskers of Mr. Natural himself, tickling me here and there? In other words, will my image of you at this moment manage to overcome those other images in my own personal scrapbook of discomfort, or will it drown in them, as have so many others, another tiny ocean liner fallen victim to the icebergs which still float there? I mean," Emily paused, "everything does come back, doesn't it?"

Yet when I came out from the small treatment room, where I was doused with some sort of antibiotic spray and Mercurochrome, Greta was gone. There were the same unhappy sick as I remembered before going in, the same easy-to-wipe-free-of-germs red plastic chairs, and the same Icelandic edition of *People* magazine, but no Greta.

"Say," I said to an orderly who was trying to work out a chess problem using various sizes of syringes on a hand-drawn board, "you haven't by any chance see a striking blond, possibly covered with soot, around here, have you?"

He shook his head, no.

Suddenly another man appeared holding a clipboard and a stethoscope. "Come this way!" he said. "You appear to be fine, but there are a few more tests we'd like to give you!"

I returned to the examining room with him, where he did this and that.

"Well!" he said, after a thorough examination. "You seem perfectly all right to me! Now I'm not saying there's nothing wrong, you understand, particularly with the history you have described! But according to all my tests you check out perfectly! Sometimes things like that just happen, and I'm sure you know medicine still does not have all the answers! It's very possible your recent fall was the necessary trigger to set off some kind of healing process beyond the scope of modern medicine! So good-bye! Good luck!" He explained that he had learned his strangely enthusiastic brand of English by reading American comic books, and called for someone to find me a spare suit of clothes.

I stood there, shivering just a little, alone and confused, and in retrospect, oddly happy, for although I did not realize it at the time, it was that very moment I began my residence on that oxymoron of a continent (or was it an island?), a world of perpetual light (in June) and perpetual dark (December), sometimes called the "Land of Fire and Ice," and which, although named "Iceland" by an early settler, reportedly depressed by seeing the waters around it so choked with ice, was actually warmer than most places at a similar latitude, a place where most residents made their living, as Sonny and Dane had told me earlier, on fish and fish-related products, with woolen sweaters as a backup. When the clothes arrived and I was driven back to my hotel room, I was pleased to learn that the publicly funded health system extended to visitors as well as natives (another plus!).

The following morning, back at my, and formerly Leo's, hotel (his last legacy was to have paid the bill early, thank goodness), the phone rang. I wondered for a moment who it could be — possibly the man from Volcano Tours, I thought — but it was Greta.

"How are you feeling after yesterday?" she asked.

"Not too bad," I said. "How about you?"

"Oh," Greta said. "I'm not feeling too bad either, except for a few sore places where I must have hit wrong. And of course I feel terrible about the death of your companion."

"Oh yes," I said. "Leo. I know what you mean, but he was really more of a fairly new friend I had come to grow quite fond of, though naturally I feel bad too."

"Well anyway," Greta said, "while you were being treated back in the emergency room, I read an article one of the doctors must have left out that explained how the best way to treat a traumatic experience was to repeat it as soon as possible, but under safe conditions. And this morning it just occurred to me that I have a small sauna in the back of my apartment building, and it might be a good idea if you came over and we recreated that hot and cold business of the volcano. I think we can skip the ash, but if you'd like, I can set some old newspapers on fire. In any case, I feel partly responsible for what happened, and I'd like to make it up to you."

It may have been the antibiotics I'd gotten the night before, or my overstressed imagination, but suddenly Greta's voice sounded huskier than it had before she inhaled all those cinders. "Oh," I said truthfully, "I'd like that. How do I get there?"

Greta answered her door wearing a short black velvet dress and fishnet stockings made (she told me later) from real fishnets. She looked recovered, and except for a massive bruise over much of her left side, her skin seemed to have healed. I decided that either she had an extraordinary immune system, or what I had mistaken for abrasions, had been only smears of lava dust. "Yesterday was quite a day," I told her.

But instead of answering, Greta only stared at me, breathing deeply, as if the very sight of Yours Truly had filled her with such a recurrence of trauma she could not speak. I took advantage of her silence to look around her apartment. On one wall was a poorly printed litho of Munch's *Scream,* and opposite it was a enlarged photo of a white and fluffy baby seal, its skin mercifully intact. There was a vase of Iceland poppies, and a wooden box piled with cassettes. Almost despite myself I looked around for signs of a boyfriend or live-in lover, but saw none. Clearly this was just the apartment of a young woman, clean but not fastidious, pleasant but not over-decorated. Then underneath a coffee table I spotted something familiar.

"Is that a portable typewriter down there?" I asked. "And if so, is it by any chance an Adler?"

"Why, 'yes' to both of your questions," Greta said. "I got it as a graduation present from high school."

"Well," I said, "it may interest you to know that the Adler was a little-known brand of superior quality that had its origins in Germany, and enjoyed a reputation for solid workmanship and close tolerances. Do you mind if I inspect it?"

She nodded, looking somewhat puzzled at the turn the conversation had taken.

I opened the case. The machine was in surprisingly good condition, except for the fact that the plastic body which housed the mechanism was cracked. "How did this happen?" I asked. "Did someone throw it?"

Greta shifted back and forth on her fishnetted legs, then sank back into the couch. "I give up," she said. "You're too good. Actually, I left it outdoors in the cold one winter and brought it inside too quickly. I wish I knew how to fix it, but I may have to give it away."

I studied it. It was a problem I had never met with in St. Nils, but I had an idea. "You don't happen to have a little flour, some food coloring, and ordinary furniture glue lying around?" I said.

"As a matter of fact I went to the store yesterday," Greta said, "and I think I do."

She returned with the items and I went to work, mixing them with my fingers into a paste fine enough to bind the cracks on the plastic shell, and asked for a butter knife. When she produced one, I pressed the mixture into the opening and, with a wet sponge, wiped off the excess. The food coloring had only been to match it to the original. "Now we'll just have to wait and see what happens," I said.

The sauna, the use of which, Greta told me, was included in her lease, was housed in a small shed behind her apartment building, and was a humble building made of corrugated metal and cedar. It was empty when we arrived, and Greta led me inside, and flipped on a switch to start the steam. Then she sat down, and began to pull off her stockings.

"You'd better undress, too," she said, "unless you want those clothes of yours completely ruined."

I did as she asked, and stacked them on a small bench outside. Greta bolted the door after us. "Don't worry," she said. "They'll be all right. As you have already heard, in Iceland we have one of the lowest crime rates in the world."

I stared at her. Even with the bruise, she was beautiful, and the purplish discoloration over so much of her body set off, in a way, the creamy texture of the rest of her skin with its fine golden hairs.

"That was quite a job you did on my typewriter a minute ago," she said. "You really do know your stuff."

Then a strange thing happened. As I explained to Greta the rigorousness of my training and the perfectionism of my teacher, somehow, like a small spark that spreads into a raging prairie fire, my passion for typewriters seemed to excite Greta as well. One thing led to another, and another, and soon we were making love, our cries of pleasure combining with the hiss of steam and the rattling of the door by Greta's neighbors wishing to use the sauna.

When we emerged at last, breathless and flushed, I was relieved to see my clothes were still there.

"See," Greta said. "I promised. Now, let's see how that typewriter turned out."

It was perfect except for a slight dullness to the surface of the filler, and I resolved to try adding a little cornstarch to the mixture in the future. "Excuse me for asking," I said, "but does this sort of thing happen very often here in Iceland?"

Greta blushed. "Yes," she said, "I'm afraid so. When you combine our high literacy rate and relatively low technological quotient, the result is that we are practically the typewriter capital of the world. And people are always lending them back and forth, leaving them out on porches and in driveways. I can probably think of a half dozen machines that have the same kind of cracks as mine had, but until now no one's known what to do about the problem. If you lived here, you could make quite a good living."

Back in Greta's apartment, the healing process continued, and the next morning Greta had a taxi go to the hotel to bring my bags to her apartment. After that, things moved quickly. Next, following another sauna (far from being traumatic, I was beginning to quite enjoy them) Greta took me shopping for clothes and I bought an Icelandic dictionary. That afternoon, back at Greta's, I rested on the couch and studied the Icelandic language, which turned out to be surprisingly easy to learn. By six that evening Greta had called around to a few of her friends and rounded up eleven broken typewriters, one of them a nifty Underwood. In other words, not only had I fallen in love with Greta, but also with the whole of this plucky, though somewhat chilly republic to the north.

How was this possible? I asked myself, even then. Was this change of plans on my part a sign of fickleness, the stigmata of some supreme lack of faithfulness, or simply the recognition of a greater principle, that of the equality of all mankind? If my attachment to Emily (which in fact had not gone away, but had merely been displaced) was instant and arbitrary, so was my attachment to Greta. Should I give up the bird in the hand for the one in the bush? Or should I consider my so-called chosen path in life as only one of a myriad of possibilities, not one of which should be privileged above any other? In short, was I a shallow playboy and out for a good time, or just a guy unusually blessed with the ability to love?

And love I did. In what seemed no time at all, I was practically a native, celebrating Iceland's Independence Day on June sixteenth of every year, and bellying up to the bar with the other natives on the twenty-fifth anniversary of the 1977 World Trade Agreement which upheld Iceland's right to claim its two-hundred-mile fishing limit. On weekends, I found myself becoming not only the lover of Greta, exploring the body of my beloved and traveling over those sweet contours as an explorer, but also a lover of that brown, stunted land, twelve percent of which I learned was more or less permanently covered by ice, and an equal amount by lava. Soon I found myself happily lost in groves of spindly birches and sickly willows, or freezing with a boot full of icy water as if I'd been born on that very spot. Or, alternatively, I would be hiking along, but then a few hundred yards in one direction or another, would find my way barred by a swift-moving, very short river, possibly flowing for no more than eighty or ninety feet before it disappeared behind a rock or underneath a gnarled stump.

And as for Leo's body, though it was the object of a brief, half-hearted search by members of Iceland's crack Tourist Rescue Squad, to no one's surprise, it was never recovered.

Then a few years passed. Greta and I became the proud parents of two children, Ingo and Inga. Ingo's hair was blond, like his mother's, and Inga's was brown, like mine. Ingo had the endearing mannerism of snuggling his head beneath a parent's arm and chirping like a young puffin, a behavior he had once witnessed on a school hike by the seashore and which had inexplicably stuck with him. Inga had an endearing mannerism of whistling snatches of classical music when she was fearful — she preferred Bach and Debussy, but had been known to do musical comedy, Rodgers and Hart being her favorite. Ingo had the annoying habit of snuffling and wiping his nose on a sleeve, not necessarily his own (shades of Leo!), whenever he failed to understand a question, and Inga had the rather upsetting habit of coughing and then falling to the ground in a fit of choking when she found herself overcome by confusion. Does this seem a hurried, and a bit of a cursory description to give of my own children, who after all were so dear to me? It is, and you will just have to trust me that the feelings I have for my entire family are far from hurried. If I hurry here (and I do), it is only to shorten the pain that accompanies these thoughts, and what in the end became my tragedy.

The typewriter repair business prospered, as Greta had said it would. I rented a small office in the center of Reykjavik, and was prosperous enough to hire an assistant, named Snori, whom I trained in the art of typewriter repair much as the old Dutchman had trained me, minus a few methods which my enlightened new home had outlawed years ago. I developed a regular clientele, and in addition took on a small stock of stationery and typewriter ribbons, even ballpoint pens, which supplemented my profits. I was happier than I had ever been. And although I didn't dare to say it out loud, my organ never felt better. It was just possible, I began to speculate, that there was something about the mostly cold climate which might have reversed the orgagenic disintegration business.

So each night I returned from my shop, the tips of my fingers black and red with the ink of typing ribbons. After walking to the kitchen where I would scrub my hands in a mixture of kerosene and cleanser (Greta hated smudges) I would go off to where one of the children was playing (for some strange reason, they never played together) and tousle his or her hair. Then I would walk around the apartment (it was small, only three rooms, but it was amazingly easy to lose each other) until I found either Greta or the missing child. Then I would tousle any remaining hair, and together as a family we would gather in the living room where I would tell them a story, a different one each evening, of how I grew up on a ranch. Dropping to my hands and knees, I would re-enact the role of Dominique with the children as the cowboys. Finally, after I had finished riding around the living room, bumping against the furniture and bucking to unseat them, the game would end with Dominique ordering them to clean their rooms and begin their homework. Greta seldom participated in these activities, but watched, knitting heavy sweaters for the coming winter, and cheered us on.

At last, when the children were exhausted from their cleaning and their studying, they would lie on our clean living room rug as Greta prepared supper and I read the newspaper. I loved Greta, of course, and yet I must admit I took a guilty pleasure in searching for news from St. Nils, perhaps in the hope that one day I might see Emily's name included. The closest I had ever come was one day finding a brief clipping that indicated St. Nils had been the epicenter of a medium-sized earthquake. I put the paper down, the children stretched safely before me. I imagined the water sloshing against the sides of the pool, and the sudden panic that the organs must have felt to have their safe world so rocked like that. Had Emily helped them, or even been there at the time? I hoped for their sake she had.

Afterwards we would go into the kitchen to eat our supper. Following supper, while Greta cleaned the dishes the children did homework, I would complete various small projects around the house such as repairing faucets or cleaning the gutters (not so easy, by the way, in total darkness). I'd do that for about an hour, then Greta and I would bathe the children and read to them from their favorite Eddas or sagas (I could never keep straight which was which, but Greta and the kids seemed to have no problem). Finally together we would tuck the children into bed.

So the days passed, filled with joys and sorrows. Or to be exact, in later years I calculated that I'd had seven hundred and twelve days of joy, and six hundred and fifty-nine days of sorrow, plus ten and a half days of grief. Also two days of hunger and seventeen full of nausea, which I attributed to Greta's penchant for trying out new recipes. In addition there were about a thousand days I'd have to call a wash — where I wasn't sure exactly what was going on. Nor could I begin to guess what Greta's own tally would look like, but of course I hoped that she was happy. Then the tragedy I mentioned earlier struck, not all at once, as in the movies, but slowly, insidiously, and creepily.

One evening at dinner after a particularly vigorous game of cowboys and pony, I noticed that Ingo was unusually apathetic to one of his favorite meals: Kod-ka-bobs, which Greta prepared by soaking cubed pieces of cod in aquavit for several hours before putting them on skewers alternating with chunks of root vegetables and onions. These she brushed with melted butter and placed beneath the broiler until they were golden brown. Also, Ingo had been falling off my back that evening more than usual. I put a hand to Ingo's forehead. The boy was burning up.

Quickly Greta and I carried him to bed and called the doctor, who was gone for the weekend, having left a number on his answering service that would not answer. Ingo's temperature rose, then rose still higher, and nothing we tried seemed to help.

"Mommy, Daddy, I'm thirsty," Ingo kept saying, but when we gave him water, he pushed it away and turned his head toward the Star Wars poster on the wall.

Finally, out of desperation, at about three in the morning, Greta and I took the child outside and rolled him around in the snow for a while. Mercifully, his fever dropped. We took him back into the house, blue and covered with goose bumps, laid him on towels, dried him off, and put him to bed, where he fell into a deep sleep. I was exhausted and I was sure Greta was too. We crawled wearily into our own bed, and just before I was about to fall asleep myself, I reached for Greta's hand and took it in mine. Greta held it half-heartedly for a moment, then let go.

"Greta," I said in a way that I hoped would not alarm her, "even with the scare over Ingo, you seem a little quiet this evening. There isn't anything else wrong, is there?"

"Oh," she replied. "Not much, I suppose, but for the past two or three years I've been feeling I should do something with my life. After all, you've got your work repairing typewriters.

You have your camaraderie with your loyal customers and your celebrating what used to be my personal national holidays. If you remember, I did have a career in the music business before I met you, and though I've been forbidden ever to work as a guide again, I had that going too. I don't really blame you, and I'm not exactly complaining, but all I ever get to do is stay home and take care of the children. I do love them, of course; it just seems like there should be more. But instead, like tonight, my life just goes on reeling from one crisis to another. Ingo is fine now, and of course I'm happy, but next week it will be Inga, and then Ingo again after that."

"I see your point," I said. "Is there anything I can do? I confess I hadn't realized you were so troubled."

"Well, it so happens that there is," she said. "I've been thinking how each night we read the children sagas and Eddas before they go to sleep, but have you noticed that none of them are by women? What kind of an example is that? What kind of a message are we giving the next generation, particularly Inga, but also Ingo, because it adds to the general misconception of seeing all women in subservient roles? It's true that in Iceland we have a woman President, but as you know the post is largely symbolic, and I worry that we're sending the wrong sort of signals to our kids, what with your own successful business and me stuck in the kitchen."

It was late, and I was very tired, but I could completely sympathize with her reasoning. "You're right, of course," I said. "But what do you propose we do?"

"As a matter of fact, I've been looking into it lately," Greta said. I could see that even as weary as she was, just talking about it created a sort of new lightness in her being that allowed her to bear things a while longer, and her face became flushed with excitement. Outside, I could hear the creak of ice shifting and the howl of the wind combine to produce a sound that was a sort of an eerie creaking whoosh, as if something old were passing away.

"There's a night-school course in Saga Writing being offered at the university, and though all of the students at present are males, mostly fishermen and members of the soccer team and so on, I was thinking of enrolling. Then if, by some chance, I'm able to write a really good saga, people could read it, and it would offer a new model of behavior for young men and women growing up that would at least be an alternative to our present, male-dominated national literature, one that would elbow aside the usual hero-centered narrative with one not only less obliged to parrot the hollow values of the patriarchy, but one which could offer as a possible substitution for those bankrupt notions the still-vibrant power of the matriarchy, with its multiple perspectives and several points of view. In other words, Paul, I'd like to try to write a saga that, instead of portraying the mythical adventures of a lone hero, would have more of a sense of give and take, compromise, and social interaction. It would present a world of shared responsibility: one that includes disappointment, and perhaps even some humor. In short, it might present a model for a success that, while less ambitious than the previous doom-centered ones, might on the other hand be more achievable."

Lying there with Greta in the dark, listening to the distant bark of harbor seals as their sound joined the creaking howling whooshing sounds already out there, I slowly took in Greta's words. I replayed them over in my mind, but even before I had a chance to digest her content, Greta continued, and, like a mountainside of snow that has sat motionless too long over the winter, but now with spring thaw rushes down the mountain in a sort of avalanche, so did her speech tumble forward.

"I have in mind," Greta said, "a setting for my new saga that is not remote or forbidding as in the past, but familiar — one of a neighborhood tavern, for example, like the one you yourself sometimes stop in after a day's work. I would name it 'Skoal!' and my saga will have not one, but several heroes, each representing a different level of society. There might be a fisherman, for instance, and perhaps a typewriter repair man (they say write about what you know), a mailman, an out-of-work salesman, and maybe even a psychiatrist. Also, unlike the traditional saga, I see women playing a major role as well, perhaps as a barmaid or even part-owner. They could provide a wry counterpoint to the usual male smugness. What do you think?"

"That's a great idea," I said, because it sounded like a sure-fire hit to me. "And if it's necessary for you to take this course so that you can succeed in writing a saga such as this, then I think you should enroll as quickly as possible."

So it was decided, and while Greta prepared to write her saga, I, unbeknown to myself, had just begun the first act of the tragedy that was to follow. As soon as the next term of the university rolled around, Greta found herself sitting at a seminar table with five rugged soccer players, plus her instructor, who, she told me, looked as if he had been a serious soccer player himself at one time, but from whom several decades of bookish concentration had sapped much energy. Class was at night — no small matter when the nights were that long. Still, as much as I had complete faith in Greta's vision, even I was surprised at the rapidity of her progress.

Soon the ritual developed that before she left for class each evening Greta would read me what she'd written earlier that day. Rather than attempting her magnum opus immediately, as I had guessed she might, Greta surprised me by beginning with a sort of warm-up, a saga about a female news anchor and the difficulties involved with the production of her show. It met, she said, with remarkable success. But then, as Greta began her work on what she called "The Big One," she became unusually private. "I've found it dissipates the flow of my creative juices if I talk about it. Old Karl" (which is how she referred to her instructor) "says I should keep it bottled up inside as long as possible, then at the last possible moment, let it explode onto the paper. Old Karl," she told me, "says he's noticed a real difference in the level of my intensity now, as compared to those nights I read it before class to you. It was his idea for me to stop, and he said he was sure you'd understand. Old Karl said to tell you I have real promise."

Little by little, the nights grew longer, until around the holidays I barely saw anything at all of Greta. She would fly through the house, pick up Inga and give her a hug, pat Ingo on his head, strew around a few presents she'd bought somewhere, and then go out again. Then one morning over breakfast, in the middle of a conversation, her hand flew up to her neck to cover some bruises.

"Gosh," I said. "What happened to your neck?"

"Oh," she said, as if she were embarrassed, "I was trying on a necklace, and it got stuck."

"How could a necklace get stuck?" I asked. "I've never heard of that."

But Greta must not have heard me, because she had already turned around to wash up a stack of dishes that had been sitting in the sink a while. Then she was out the door.

At last we passed the winter solstice, and with the light growing to three and a half hours a day, I expected things to get better. But even though I managed to avoid bringing up the forbidden subject of her saga's progress, things didn't really change. Finally I stopped Greta on the way to her class one evening. Inga, who had been spending longer and longer periods of time sitting in her corner, her arms wrapped about herself and rocking from side to side, was starting to look like she might be a good candidate for long-term psychiatric care. "I don't know if more sunlight would help or if maybe we should . . ." I began, but before I could finish, Greta burst into tears.

"You've been so good, and so helpful, and so dumb," she said. "I don't know how to tell you, but now I can't conceal it: Old Karl isn't nearly as old as he looks, and for the past few months before class, and after, and during class breaks, we've been having . . . well . . . I guess you'd have to call it an affair."

I was stunned. Greta's shoulders were shaking, and the heavy eye shadow she favored, a carry-over from her musical days, was smeared. "How's your saga going?" I asked.

She pulled herself together. "Very well, thank you," she answered. "I've nearly completed the first draft, and now all it needs is some polishing. You can read it after it's typed, if you like. Old Karl has promised that he'll show it to some influential editors he's acquainted with. He thinks it has real possibilities." Greta paused for a moment. "And now, I'd like a divorce."

"But I still love you," I said. "Nonetheless, I want you to know that it is not my wish to hold you back from a promising literary or any other career, if that's what you really want. But there are Ingo and Inga to think about as well," I said. "Surely we owe it to the two of them to try to make a go of it. Just the other day I saw a documentary film where a mother polar bear was shot, and the cub was left behind. It was one of the saddest things I've ever witnessed. By the way, do we have polar bears in Iceland?"

"I'm not sure," Greta replied. "There is much wisdom to what you say, but now I've got to go to class. I'll think about it."

And she did. Night after long night, as we struggled onward, not knowing whether to go or stay, to laugh or cry, to try or to give up. Thus the curtain fell on *Iceland,* Act One.

Then one day Inga, much improved after the psychological intervention we had finally decided was necessary, came home from school while I happened to be bedridden with severe bronchitis. Inga was becoming a fine girl, and also, as an extra benefit, I was relieved to see that the choking fits had mostly stopped.

"I'm trying to decide whether or not to grow breasts, Dad," she said, as she set a cup of hot tea down on my bedside table.

"Not for a while, I hope," I chuckled. Then Inga turned to leave, hesitated, and turned back again.

"Dad," she said, out of nowhere at all, "what's at the center of an ice cube?"

I must have looked puzzled, because Inga repeated her

99

question, speaking more slowly, as if to a foreigner. "If you take an ice cube, then melt it so that it somehow melts evenly on all sides, then is the very last piece of ice to disappear the center?"

"Yes," I coughed, turning my head away. I couldn't remember if bronchitis was catching.

"Then," Inga continued, "that tiny piece of ice remaining, does that have a center too?"

"Of course it does," I said.

"Then when that's gone, is the center part, or whatever part was the center, still there?"

Emily . . . I thought. Emily would enjoy this conversation.

"Is this for a science project?" I asked, "because. . . ."

"No," Inga said. "I just want to know."

"Well, OK." I said. "Then the place that was the center is there, but the center isn't."

"But if that's the case," Inga persisted, "if the center is still there, and can't be seen, what good is having a center at all?"

"Hmm," I said, and then and at that very moment two things came to me. First, that I might look into getting the dosage of Inga's medication increased, just in case, and second, that perhaps I needed to do something about Greta's unhappiness once and for all. Perhaps, it occurred to me, that the answer to everything would be for the whole family — Inga, Ingo, Greta, and me — to take an outing to some place both Greta and the children would find meaningful and fun, the sort of trip that might bind us together as a unit once again, and provide a template for our future.

That evening, when the children had gone to sleep, I told Greta my idea.

"It could work," she ventured. "At least it's a start. I don't know if I've mentioned it," she continued, "but one night a couple weeks ago after class had finished, Old Karl called me aside to say he'd lost interest in me. He said he attributed his interest in the first place to the sudden appearance of a woman in such an unfamiliar setting, and said he was going to see if the University couldn't make rules against this happening again. So Old Karl and I are history, but that doesn't exactly mean that you are I are back again, the same as before."

Still, I was encouraged. Maybe, I thought, we had a chance after all. But where could we go that would provide a sort of focusing modicum of danger, like the descent into the volcano that had made me a resident of Iceland, but without the actual fatality, of Leo, for example, that particular trip included?

Then it came to me. It might be fun for the children, as well as an encouragement to Greta's writing career, if the whole family took a trip to visit the tomb of Ragnar, possibly the greatest teller of sagas in the recent history of Icelandic literature, whose insistence on being buried in a tomb of ice in the exact center of the island was partially the reason for his notoriety.

I made a few inquiries among my customers and was told that Ragnar's Tomb, never exactly a popular tourist spot, was practically inaccessible during the spring. And while no one I spoke to had actually been there, Snori, whom I caught in the middle of a delicate job on a Smith Corona that only the day before had fallen off a fisherman's boat onto a sandbank, scoffed. "If the mud doesn't get you, the snow will. If you have to go," he said, "I'd wait until at least July."

Somehow, the man's know-it-all attitude, especially for an employee, made July seem a long way off. If there was anything Greta and I needed, it was immediate bonding.

And so began Act Two of the tragedy. The day we left home turned out to be a beautiful one, surprisingly warm for spring, and we drove most of the way with the car's windows rolled down. The children sang songs and counted barns. There were only five, and even with the long time between counts, they managed not to quarrel. Upon arriving at the base of the mountain that sheltered the earthly remains of Ragnar, I decided to park the rented car in the gravel alongside the road (there was a small spot where snowplows turned around, but that was entirely filled with a soup of brown mud). Partly to avoid lugging our heavy picnic basket all the way up the mountain, we voted to eat our lunch by the car, a rattling Ford Escort. So Greta spread a wool blanket on the hood of the car and we all stood around as if we had come to a rustic lunch counter, eating our fish sandwiches, pickles, chips, and cake and drinking sodas. The adventure, I was foolish enough to believe, was beginning well.

There was no traffic on the road alongside us — people were right about the lack of visitors — and very little wind. Above me I could hear the squawk of birds returning from wherever they'd spent their winter, and in the distance a faint roar that I guessed might be the call of a mating polar bear.

"Greta," I asked, "did you ever have the chance to find out whether Iceland had polar bears?"

"No," she said somewhat snappishly. "I've been too busy writing my saga, but if it was so important to you, why didn't you look it up yourself?"

Frankly I'd hoped for a little more understanding at that point, but I also knew that her request was not unreasonable, so I remained silent. Then we washed our plates in a brownish drift of snow and returned them, cold, to the basket, which I lifted back into the Escort's trunk. At last we began the climb up the narrow trail that led to our destination.

Without ever having seen it, or even any pictures, I suddenly realized that in my imagination I had pictured this lofty grave, carved out of the heart of a glacier, as being diamond-like, and sparkling with light, or at the very least like one of those clear joke ice cubes with a fly (in this case, Ragnar) suspended in the center. But as is so often the case, reality was not at all like that. Instead of the crystal lineaments I had fantasized, the entrance to Ragnar's icy tomb looked more like any other cave I'd seen — and I'd seen plenty in my wanderings — with no monument other than a simple plywood sign stuck into the wet, brown earth and shaped like an arrow. It read: "Ragnar — this way." Seeing it, I felt two emotions: first, I was relieved to know that we were on the right track direction-wise; and second, I was saddened by the transitory nature of fame and its rewards.

And yet, of course, in this instance, as in the events that followed, there was no one to blame but me. I realized that if I'd just taken a few minutes beforehand to think about the nature of glaciers I'd already seen, I wouldn't have been so mistaken. Of course any great mass of ice that had been alternately receding and advancing for centuries, plowing through dirt and leaving more of it behind, had to wind up covered with debris. So instead of some sort of brilliant jewel set in the center of a transparent gothic cathedral, with light streaming in from towering windows and bouncing off tricky vaulted ceilings, the tomb of Ragnar was absolutely dark, or would have been without the single lightbulb plugged into an extension cord which ran outside to somewhere.

The bulb, screwed into one of those wire-covered baskets mechanics use to work on cars, was hung exactly above the coffin in the center of the enormous room, and the mesh protected the bulb from the dirt and such that dropped from the ceiling every ten seconds or so. Nor was this debris, I observed, merely harmless pebbles. Studding both the ceiling and the walls were rocks which ranged in size from marbles to regulation bowling balls, one of which, in effect, welcomed us as we walked in by popping off a wall and rolling up to us, like a friendly pup, before it came to a halt a few feet away. I looked up to see several grapefruit-sized chunks protruding from the ceiling above us, and moved to a safer spot.

Still, the bare bulb, the coffin, and the cold, combined with the danger of the stones — all of these together created, almost despite themselves, the exact kind of noble eternal moment one might expect from the bard who had written the lines: "And so he slipped to the ground with a thud / his nose and mouth filled mostly with blood." The key word, Greta said, being "mostly." These lines, Greta informed us, were from Ragnar's greatest work, "The Einar Saga," four scenes of which were carved out of the ice of the glacier itself, one per wall, and which surrounded the forever-dozing bard.

And indeed, Ragnar himself, now long past caring about the vicissitudes of meter or of gravity, was an impressive sight. There he lay on a block of ice, perfectly preserved by the cold, a tall man, with beady blue eyes, wiry dark hair and a long — far too long — upper lip which culminated in a far too blubbery mouth. Though his dark Italian suit was spotted with the debris that had dropped from the ceiling, he still clutched in his heavy frozen fist the same trademark shiny black legal briefcase in which he kept his poems while he was alive. Indeed, Ragnar still gave off the same air of frozen dignity, it seemed to me, as he had throughout his life in Iceland, where he was known as much for his refusal to assume the trappings of Bohemia as for his poems themselves. "Dress for success" Greta quoted him to the three of us as we quietly stared at the sleeping bard, "and you can forget the rest."

Now there he was dressed for success for all eternity, stubbornly planted in the center of this glacier in the center of his native land, surely having been aware that the dangers of falling boulders and seas of mud would keep all but the hardiest pilgrims, such as our small foursome, away. I turned to Greta to see if she could offer any additional insight about this powerful personality, but she was preoccupied, possibly by measuring the place of women in general in the history of Icelandic literature, and of her own work in particular.

So I examined the four murals carved from ice that surrounded the endless-night-inhabiting maker of sagas as behind me I heard the aimless kicking of children's boots against the walls. Perhaps, it occurred to me, I might find a detail from one of them that Greta could use for her own inspiration. I looked at the tableaux around me. Each depicted a scene from the life of Einar, the autobiographical hero of Ragnar's epic work. One picture was at his left, one at his right, with one at his head and the last at his feet.

In the first (going clockwise from his head), the saga's hero, Einar, sat on the couch in his living room, his stocking feet propped up on a coffee table covered with what looked to be periodicals of one sort or another. As he rested, I could see, thanks to one of those devices also used in theater sets where a wall of a house has been removed to show what's outside, a young neighbor girl knocking at his door. She had brought with her a large bag, and judging by its weight, it was full of sample Christmas cards to sell, even though Christmas was a long way off. The girl, whose name (through a typical male oversight, Greta said) was never revealed in the poem, was nubile and naïve, and trying to save enough money to buy a puppy she had seen in a pet shop window. So in this first illustration of the saga, she had put down the heavy sample bag to ring his doorbell. And at that moment, uncertain of how she would be received, she looked both touching and vulnerable, thanks to the skill of the artist.

"And no wonder she is frightened," I remarked in an ill-timed attempt to lighten the atmosphere of the place, "because such a practice as selling greeting cards door-to-door has been abandoned years ago by most other civilized countries of the world."

Greta, however, refused to be drawn into my banter, and the children were off busy in one corner carving their initials into a wall of ice.

In the next scene, the one to Ragnar's left, Einar had invited the girl inside, and the two were sitting at his kitchen table, from which he had removed his supper: a loaf of bread, and what was either an especially large apple or a small head of cabbage. Her card samples were spread out upon its surface, and by the light of an old-fashioned lantern, Einar studied them to determine which illustration would best express his personality: heroic, but shy and sensitive to the opinions of others. He appeared to be leaning in favor of a fishing scene — a boat with lights strung in the shape of a Christmas tree from its mast.

The boat was struggling to return home, possibly on Christmas Eve, through a stormy sea, and far above it was a star, the star of Christmas. Meanwhile the yellow light of the lantern on the table beautifully illuminated the innocent face of the young neighbor girl from beneath, and the tips of her thin shoes just barely touched the heavy, fur-lined boots of Einar.

The third scene, the one Ragnar's feet were pointing toward, had Einar looking over the cards he just received from the greeting card company. It was clear, even through the imperfect medium of ice-carving, that they were poorly printed, and on cheap paper, but they had arrived none too soon, for the Christmas holiday was approaching. Oblivious to their lack of quality, the neighbor girl, who Einar had invited in to see the actual product, was playing with her new puppy on the floor. Seeing her joy, Greta explained that it was hard for Einar to resent the cruel exploitation of such children by greedy corporations. Already he had given her an endearing nickname, and made her a little cot in the corner, so that when she came home from school in the future and found no one home at her own house, she could come to Einar's and rest until her parents arrived. "They'll come home pretty soon / and if they don't / you can play with my balloon," Greta quoted.

Finally, the last tableau illustrated the last section of the poem, which was, Greta said, essentially just a meditation on the transitory and often disappointing nature of human existence. On his way to the post office to get his cards in the mail in time, Einar, driving his rusted Buick Roadmaster, had run over the girl's puppy, which lay motionless near the front wheel of the large and heavy car. In the poem, Greta said, Einar, in a sudden fit of depression and remorse, asked himself whether or not he would be better off just to renounce this world once and for all. And yet if he did, she explained, we know from the extended soliloquy that forms the poem's final stanzas, that to renounce a world without meaning would be to make a gesture in itself equally without meaning. As Einar said, if "this world one day will melt / like an ice cube in the night / then what's the point of being right?" Next to him, the girl, her trust in her neighbor completely shattered along with her faith in the power of being an entrepreneur, kneels staring at her lifeless dog.

"No kidding," I said, and made a promise to myself that I would read the entire saga the minute we got home.

And so the visit of this/our/my small family to this great bard came to an end. As Ingo poked a stick into one of Ragnar's frozen nostrils while Greta wrested it away from him, I announced, "It's time for us to leave." We exited the cave in a scuffle of snow gear, and I tried to take Greta's hand in order to begin our healing process as quickly as possible. Greta, however, was wearing heavy gloves, and, possibly not feeling my touch, she pulled away. Maybe she was right, I decided, if any meaningful change was to come, it would have to come slowly, and the process would have to be as gradual as that which had brought about the need for it in the first place. It would emulate not the swiftness of a bolt of lightning, but instead, a glacier's slow creep forward on rollers of crushed ice.

But I was wrong again.

We were about halfway down the mountain, when the third and final act of *Iceland* began. No longer, I was sorry to say, were we the tight family unit we had been when we had been struggling up the muddy path to the tomb. Walking back to the road, we were spread apart, a straggly line with the children running ahead, oblivious to my shouts for them to slow down, and Greta shuffling far behind me, absorbed, I supposed, in her thoughts of a creative and personal nature. And it was then that I detected, dully at first, through my fuzzy green earmuffs, one of the most frightening sounds I had ever heard in my entire life, and if I had not been wearing the muffs pressed so tightly into my ears as to be almost painful, I imagine that it would be even more frightening. It began as a whisper, though without any actual words, then more like a shush, the sound of a mother, though some gigantic matriarch, to be sure, bent over a feverish child, not wanting to wake him, but merely to signal her presence and to give him comfort. Next, as if slowly bending her head to his, until her lips nearly touched the sick child's burning ear, the mother still continued to make that awful soothing sound, until the noise grew louder, grew deafening.

I took off my earmuffs and looked around, confused. Then I saw it: a white spume of snow, as magnificent and wild as the mane of a white horse, rising against the blue of the spring sky until it overwhelmed the whole horizon, turning the heavens at first white, then, gray, then nearly black. The sound belonged, of course, to an avalanche.

"Greta!" I yelled, and my voice disappeared into the then ultra-deafening shush of the snow as if it had been sopped up by gigantic wads of cotton. "Ingo! Inga!" And in reply, I heard nothing but the gigantic hush, horribly descending.

Instinctively, I dived beneath a narrow rock outcropping that jutted out at my right, and lay there trembling, scarcely daring to breathe as bushes, branches, whole trees, boulders, and something that might even have been a polar bear but was traveling so fast I couldn't be certain, all passed over me. Then it went completely and absolutely dark. All I could feel was the ground, along with every cell of my body, rumbling in the general movement of snow, and sky, and earth.

Then everything was quiet. Miraculously, the rock I had huddled behind had withstood the force of the wave of snow, and though I was buried beneath I knew not how many feet of white powder (and I never did find out), at least I was able to tell which direction was up. Thus it was I began to claw, dig, and fumble my way to freedom, slowly, painfully, inch by inch and foot by foot, toward the world of men and loss, and loss, and loss, once more.

IV

In the end, all I could really do was to take care of business. I stood around like a dolt, stamped my feet in the snow to warm them, and watched helplessly as little by little it became clear that the rescue operation, as earnest as it was, was going to fail. I gave the required benumbed interviews to the media. I presided over a memorial service at my children's school, during which their still-living classmates presented me with a small stack of carefully printed farewell letters, complete with brightly colored drawings, each one declaring how much they would miss their special friends. Then, escorted by their respective teachers, I emptied the contents of my children's still-unoccupied desks into a two large brown paper bags, and carried them home, where they squatted in a corner of my kitchen, accusing, horrible, and in fact the size of two small children.

I took long walks, but the landscape I had so delighted in previously succeeded only in making me feel like an accomplice. I went to work each day, half-heartedly. I used part of the proceeds from the insurance policy that Greta had insisted I buy, to move out of our old apartment into one without so many painful memories. None of it helped. When the country a person lives in is so small that every street corner and every shop has already been associated with the events of a life, and even the very words everyone speaks are in the language of those you love, there is no getting away.

I tried to stay, but failed. I sold the shop to a grateful Snori, and the next day bought a plane ticket back to St. Nils. I sat silently, as a motherly flight attendant, evidently having seen one of my television interviews, bumped me up to first class and offered me an extra chocolate tart ("Just in case," she said slyly). And I had lost the emotional resilience to resist.

Then, following the appropriate number of connecting flights and delays in airport terminals, at last I stepped into the bright, warm sunlight of St. Nils, and wept as my shabby suitcases, stuffed with the pain-laden detritus of the past seven years, clunked down the conveyor belt like a recurring nightmare. Not knowing what else to do, I visited my former landlord to see if he had any rentals available at the moment, and also to belatedly apologize for having left without having given any notice other than the letter I had sent him from Iceland, along with an announcement of my wedding. Sitting at my landlord's kitchen table, I found myself weeping once again.

"I'm sorry," I said. "Maybe it was a mistake to come back."

But my former landlord was a gentleman. He said he hadn't been inconvenienced in the least by my sudden departure, and the money he had gotten from my security deposit, plus the first and last month's rent, as well as selling all my clothing, furniture and old typewriters had more than made up for his trouble. He told me the prices he had gotten for several models, and I was impressed with his business acumen. He had rented the place out again, he said, almost immediately after I left, to a girl who worked at the local bookstore. And she'd been a good tenant, too, but apparently a month ago a customer stopped in her store as he was looking for a book on sexually transmitted diseases. One thing led to another, the landlord reported she had told him, and now she was living with the man in his luxury condo overlooking the harbor. "So it's your good luck," he said. "I was just about to offer it for rent again, but it's yours if you want it." Then he added, almost as an afterthought, "Oh, and I've kept a letter that arrived after you left. You were already in Iceland by then, but it came in a large brown envelope that smelled of perfume. I thought it might be important, so I saved it."

The landlord disappeared momentarily inside a walk-in closet behind his desk, and emerged with a dusty plain manila envelope and a couple of keys. "Here," he said. "You can start moving in tomorrow."

I took the letter with me to the Motel 6 where I'd been staying, and lay down with it on the light blue bedspread. The envelope still smelled faintly of flowers, and, given the fragile mood I was in, I wasn't quite sure I wanted to open it. I stared at the lime green curtains of the room, and out at the world beyond them, and then looked back again. It wasn't just that I was holding an unopened piece of mail, but a whole other life entirely, one that had been stillborn, and which I could attempt to resurrect, or not. I wasn't sure I had the energy left, in a way, to try again. I got up, went outside to the soft drink dispenser, took a diet black cherry soda from it back to my room, looked out the window again, and then back, then out, and back. At last I opened the soda, then the letter. It was handwritten, not typed, and the ink that had been used could not have been too permanent; the past several years had turned it a light brown.

My Darling Paul,

You were here, and now you're gone, and it seems like a cruel dream, or would be if I was not absolutely certain that I will be seeing you again any day now.

(So the letter began, in a hand that was fond of large looping capitals, and i's made of little circles. Suddenly it occurred to me to wonder how on earth Emily could have found where to deliver it, when she hadn't known my last name. Was it possible that in addition to her other qualities, Emily was either a gifted sleuth [maybe she had tracked me down through Dr. Pearlman], or that she possessed abilities of a psychic nature? It was even a possibility, I guessed, that the envelope I had just opened had been a part of a mass delivery to everyone in St. Nils named "Paul." I pushed that troubling thought out of my mind. Maybe I'd mentioned fixing typewriters at one time or another in a quiet moment, in which case finding my address would have been comparatively easy.)

I don't know what came over me the other day at the pool. To put it simply, I'm not usually so forward, or dare I say, aggressive, but there was something about seeing you there, so sincere, so confused, really — and then, on top of it, you needed an organ — that completely overwhelmed me. To make matters worse, I even forgot to ask your last name, but tracked you down through the envelope you left behind with directions to the Institute. Fortunately, it had your address on it. In any case, I'm writing now to say I think I care a lot for you, but after all the near-misses I've had in the past, and after all of the losers who've taken advantage of my generous nature, for once I've decided to follow the advice of my therapist, Mitzie. "Take it slow," Mitzie is always saying, and I think you would like her. I also think she's right: this time I'd like to take some time to think before I jump into a relationship. That is, only if it's OK with you, of course (here Emily had drawn a Happy Face). But before, as Mitzie put it, I continue my old pattern of fantasy and rejection, she suggested you get to know me a little better on paper first. You already know some other things (followed by another Happy Face). Then if that doesn't scare you, you can tell me about yourself as well. So Paul, here it goes. And I hope you don't hate me. (Here she'd drawn a sad face.)

Originally, I'm from the Midwest and was raised (did I tell you this?) on a farm. While my substance-abusing parents, Lonnie and Brad, were an ordinary mom and dad in many ways, in others they weren't. Of course no child understands exactly how their parents are different than other parents when we're growing up — we're all born into life thinking everything's normal, and it's only later, when we grow up, that we start to find out things weren't. In my case, one of the things that affected me the most was my parents' telling me that I should never, ever, under any circumstances, extend my hand to be shaken by a stranger. It was weird. All around me I'd see children my own age extending their own small hands to teachers, mailmen, and their friends. They'd exchange names and say hello, often even hugging one another in the process, then they'd shake their hands and release them without any visible damage. Meanwhile I would stand there watching, trembling in the shadows, afraid to step forward and join this relaxed and untroubled society by extending my own.

"Why?" I remember thinking. So then one day when I was seven or eight, I thought I'd ask. I'd just returned home from school, and Brad was trying to put a shelf above the kitchen sink, but was having trouble getting it straight. He was yelling a lot, but I supposed it was just a way of blowing off a little steam. Also, he had gotten a dose of bad Ampicillin a couple days earlier, and some of that still must have been in his system, because he was acting really irritated. Anyway, he started to yell at me. "Of course you can't see anything. Germs are invisible, but an hour from now, a day, two days, depending on the incubation period, one of those children whose hands you watched being shaken may die, and all because of germs. But then," he continued, "as we both know, germs aren't really the issue."

As Brad carefully placed a marble on the shelf to check it for straightness, I thought about germs. The marble raced to the left and rolled under the stove. It was true, even though my parents *did* require me to wear the same disposable surgical gloves they themselves wore at home, they never insisted that I wear them in public, so they were right; germs couldn't be the issue.

"Yes," my mother chimed in. "We know how cruel children can be, and besides, we're not fanatics. We do live on a farm, after all."

This was true, of course, although I chose not to point out why.

"Yes," Brad continued, "it's not really so much the germs, though they *are* a problem. The real difficulty is the setting of the limits that follow shaking hands. That's where all the trouble tends to lie." For some reason, at that exact moment I remember he was wearing a t-shirt, rumpled boxer shorts, and monogrammed socks, and of course the rubber gloves.

"Your father's right," Lonnie said. She was always backing him up like that. Then she touched her extremely short, clean hair with one of her own gloved hands. "If a little boy takes your hand to shake it, let's just say, for the sake of argument, he extends a finger to touch you lightly on the bottom of your wrist as well. And then, if he touches you on your wrist, we have to introduce the question of where exactly your wrist ends. Suppose you tell this boy — let's call him Marty — you tell him that your wrist ends at the elbow. Then, Marty will counter by pointing out that the elbow is like the wrist in that they are both only simple hinges, devices put there only to add mobility to the arm. What can you possibly tell him then, and why shouldn't he move on?"

(If you're still with me at this point, Paul, you may notice that Lonnie had a philosophical bent I seem to have inherited.)

"And speaking of mobility, suppose that encouraged by your stumbling attempts to answer this irrefutable logic with your own, Marty then lays his child-sized hand on some other area of mobility — your shoulder, or your hip? Will Marty stop there? Why should he? What is there to stop him from reaching out one of his small fingers and beginning to stroke the tender skin at your jaw line until it tingles with pleasure, and from there, to allow his hand to travel to the base of your neck, tracing light circles around the vertebrae at the spot where your head and your spine connect? And from there, as if descending a ladder, what is there to stop that seemingly demon hand from continuing down your spine, vertebrae by vertebrae, until it reaches that last reminder of your animal nature, your tailbone itself? And then where is Marty's finger now?"

I shuddered.

"Well, I can tell you," Lonnie continued. "Right now it's too close, that's where it is, and if it's not actually in your pants, it wants to be. So then, when he asks you why not, what's wrong with going into your pants, what are you going to say? What are you going to tell Marty when he asks you if you've already let him go this far, why not farther? How are you going to answer Marty when he asks you to explain why one part of your body should be treated differently than any other? Exactly how, he'll ask, pretending to care about your answer, is your wrist different than your elbow, or your jaw, or your neck, or your spine? And when Marty evokes the ancient argument that God created us as a whole, not with some areas more important than others, what's your reply going to be then? And this," Lonnie banged the kitchen table with her fist, "is why I say to you that to say hello and to hold out your hand is nothing more or less than to give permission for yourself to be touched anywhere, at any time of the day or night, by Marty, his filthy friends, or anyone else."

Nor had she finished. "Now you might say that this is not much of a problem. You might say this because Marty is still a little boy, and because Marty's little hands, sticky with Ho Hos and Ding Dongs, and Yoo-hoos, are just a little boy's hands. You might say that even though Marty's hands may carry a germ or two, surely it is worth so little a risk to be accepted by one's schoolmates. So you might say. But listen to your mother, me, Lonnie: You just wait until Marty's little boy hands become big grown-up hands, and Marty's little boy fingers grow long and big-boy strong, and start to probe into places where they should not be. Just wait until Marty's sexual organ, still so undeveloped in the primary grades, begins to fill up with sperm, and germs, and who knows what else — Emily — you just ask your father what can happen."

(Paul, if you are still with me, I want you to know that Mitzie thinks this sort of thing is one of my issues, and the whole idea of this letter is, as she put it, "a big mistake." But I told her it was important that you know everything right from the start, that you know all the things I would have told you on our first date, if it had turned out to be a more conventional one, like a hamburger and a shake, and maybe a glass of wine. I told her that sometimes all the therapy in the world can't overrule what's in a person's heart.)

"Yes," Brad explained, "your mother is absolutely right." He sat down in the kitchen chair, and studied the shelf. The left side was definitely lower, so he took out a matchbook and slid it between the shelf and the bracket. It helped.

Then he turned to me: "And besides the matter of the touching, there is also the holding on. How long, for example," he continued, "is a handshake really? And if a brief, too-limp handshake, where the hand is merely raised once and lowered once, then released, is thought to be undesirable, it also stands to reason that a firm one, where the hand of the shakee is held tightly by the shaker, and then moved up and down not just once, but repeatedly, as if the shaker is loath to give it up and in fact is imparting some esoteric infusion of good-will into the shakee, is far more desirable. But now you see the logical trap we have created. If the harder the hand is held and the longer it is clasped the more desirable it becomes" (come to think of it, both my parents were sort of philosophers) "then what is to prevent someone, once having seized your hand, from not letting go, say, through an entire conversation, or even a dinner where both partners are therefore forced to eat using only one hand. I know this sounds awkward, and it is, but believe me, it's possible.

"And that's only the start. This Artie person. . . ."

"Marty," my mother corrected him.

"Once Marty gets hold of your hand," Brad resumed, "don't think he'll quit. Before you know it he will turn that innocent handshake into a hug, and then, from a hug, to an embrace, and then, before you know it, you'll wake up one morning to find yourself in bed underneath this Marty, his little penis already inside you, shaking up and down, and you're shaking too — you can't help it, and then you're screaming 'More,' and 'Now,' and 'Yes,' and 'Please,' and 'Oh my God,' and this Marty is still moving up and down, and so are you, and you don't even know if he's washed, and where did this start but with a so-called harmless handshake?"

Nor, Paul, will I ever forget the expression on Brad's face as he got up and began to put the hammer, screwdriver, and drill back in the box under the sink.

I put the letter down, overwhelmed, to say the least. What monsters all parents were, but especially this Brad and this Lonnie. What would it have been to be raised by such a couple, I wondered, as compared to my own days on the ranch with Dominique? Suddenly I heard a knock on the flimsy plywood door of my motel room, the sort of a door, as so many like it, that seemed to have as its entire raison d'être the certainty that it would be bashed in at one time or another. Opening it, I was surprised to see two clean-shaven young men, both in white shirts. Behind them I spotted what must have been their rusting two-wheelers bolted to the gate at the motel's office.

"Good afternoon," the taller one said. "My name is Scott, and this is Denton. We wondered if you have a few moments to spend discussing where you'll be spending eternity." Then they just stood there, oblivious of my wishes, waiting for an answer.

I explained that at that very moment I was trying to find the missing piece to a puzzle that had troubled me for several years, but which had also, in a way, led me to experiences I had never anticipated, both in St. Nils and in Iceland, from which I had recently returned. I explained to them that my own life experience had taught me that to anticipate anything, even eternity, might well be a waste of time, both of theirs and mine, and I was just getting to the part about my first visit to the organ pool when I noticed they were beginning to get nervous. Sure, I thought, I might be feeling uncomfortable, but what right did I have to make them uncomfortable as well?

"Well, OK," I said. "Suppose *you* tell *me*."

The two young men visibly relaxed, and Denton began a strange and rambling story of his own, part of which involved a prophet and a lost message much like Emily's letter. His story, however, also included an angel, and he seemed scornful of any inference that our two narratives might in any way be similar.

As he spoke, I watched him more closely. It was clear that the young man was growing more excited. He described the journey of his people through the hardships of the Midwestern United States until they reached Utah; how the grasshoppers ate their wheat and then the seagulls ate the grasshoppers, but when a few of the pioneers tried to eat the seagulls, they spit them out in disgust. He explained how many of the men took two, three, up to eight or nine wives at the same time, and how the pleasures of polygamy were greatly exaggerated by the sensationalist media.

While Denton painted this vivid, yet somehow sobering picture of the faith he was inviting me to become a follower of, Scott got up and began to pace the room, stopping every so often to look out the window, and once he took a glass from the bathroom shelf and, unwrapping its sanitary cover, poured himself a drink of water. There was no reason for me to be offended by this, as it wasn't really my home or my glass, but somehow I felt miffed.

"I'll be happy to sign off on part one," I said, "but frankly, I may be dying at this minute, and the thought of taking on a new lifestyle seems a bit too much to handle. Good-bye and good luck," I said, and they left.

After I calmed down again, I returned to Emily's letter.

There is, however, one other incident I would like to include, and this one has nothing to do with my parents. It is the one, my darling, that is the real reason I have hesitated to contact you, the one that has followed me most of my life, the single incident, by the way, above all that Mitzie advised me not to share.

It was the summer, I guess, when I was about twelve, and raising money to buy a spotted calf for a 4-H Club project by selling Christmas cards door to door. (Those were the days when kids did that sort of thing, along with paper routes and cutting lawns, but I'm afraid those times are long gone.) Anyway, it was a hot day, and walking the miles between farms wasn't easy, so when our neighbor, Farmer Wilmer, whose wife had recently passed away, invited me inside for a glass of lemonade, I accepted.

Well, Paul, one thing led to another — a story I suppose that isn't actually very new — but the end result was I got the calf, that I named Marty, and eventually he won third prize at the 4-H show. The cards, when they actually arrived, were a disappointment, but that didn't stop Farmer Wilmer from buying Marty from me when it came time to raise money for college.

Then, one of those weekends in my freshman year when I came home, I stopped by his farm to visit Marty. The calf was gone, and I saw that Farmer Wilmer got a funny look on his face, a look I had seen before on the faces of other farmers.

"You didn't," I said.

"I'm afraid so," he told me, and then had the nerve to reach out to give me a hug.

"Get away," I said, "or I'll report you to the authorities as I should have done years ago," and that was the last I saw of Farmer Wilmer, who had a stroke while pitching hay about a year later, about the time I dropped out of college.

I put the letter down once again; it now felt strangely heavy. What was Emily saying? Of course I had heard of stories like this one before — who hadn't — but Farmer Wilmer? I tried to picture the man, tall and possibly gray, in slim-fitting overalls and a rakish straw hat. Perhaps he had had one foot cocked, resting on the tire of a tractor as he watched the small girl trudging up his dusty driveway, dragging her heavy satchel behind. Had he rushed in the house and quickly squeezed some lemons, or was it merely a fortuitous stroke of luck that he had a pitcher of the stuff already chilling in the fridge, maybe next to casseroles from the funeral? What a monster! And come to think of it, the Midwest seemed to be full of them.

I picked up the remaining page, and continued.

So now, Paul, I've told you everything. Despite Mitzie's warning, I've revealed everything there is for you to know. The only thing I am doing that she suggested is that instead of rushing into yet another disastrous relationship as I have in the past, I promised her I would take two weeks off in order to let things "cool down," and also to give you a chance to respond to this letter into which I have poured (and I know it's a cliché) my entire heart. Please call me if you want to continue this relationship. If I don't hear from you in the next few days, I will assume you find me too horrible, and much too embarrassing to pursue. So this is it. This is my experiment, and if it fails, as it may well do, never again will I open my heart to another the way I have to you today in this letter.

And if you do hate me, Paul, I don't suppose I blame you, really, because for a person like yourself to be attracted to a filthy person like me would be too wonderful to believe. Nor do I want you to feel any pressure from a person like me. It's true I've tried to take my life in the past, but I am sure right now, as I write this letter, I am in a better place mentally, thanks to Mitzie. If anything should happen, an accident or some other misfortune, I don't want you to take any kind of blame.

Instead, Paul, if you hate me, I only hope you will be proud of yourself for the strength and honesty that allowed you to act according to the wisdom of your own dear heart. Know that I would not love you the way I do if I were not certain you have the courage to let a person know she is not worthy of you, or anyone, so why even keep trying.

Hoping that your organ will soon be better, I await your reply.

Sincerely,

Emily

By the following week I had moved back to my old place.

V

It may have been only my imagination, but actually it did seem that my organ *had* been beginning to act up a bit, particularly late in the evenings and between two and three in the afternoons. Despite the reassurances of that pleasant doctor back in Iceland, I was forced to admit that I was getting worried. I picked up the phone to call Dr. Pearlman, and hoped he was still in business, but the line was dead. Of course, I thought, I hadn't yet called the phone company to obtain service (I'd only moved in two days earlier). So I walked to the pay phone down by the Treasure Chest, and was told by a cheerful sounding customer service representative that it would take a week at the soonest, as the crews were currently very busy. I thanked her and returned home, where I took off my shoes and lay down. It was my hope that I'd be able to catch a few hours sleep before the next time my organ decided to call itself to my attention.

But as so often happened at stressful periods of my life, things did not go entirely as planned. As usual, in order to help me relax, I began with my favorite sleep-inducing technique, a scene that had as its actual source a ride I once took with Dominique. We had ridden over the remains of an old sod prairie hut, and together had fallen through the roof into the main room. Fortunately, neither of us were hurt, and it was no real difficulty for me to lead Dominique back up to the surface, but it got me to thinking what it would be like for the two of us to be living in a single room underground, maybe a basement, over a long period of time.

I tried it out later, the first time I left home, and found it oddly comforting. In this scenario, Dominique and I were both being held prisoner by some malignant, yet compassionate-enough-to-lower-a-basket-of-food-down-from-a-rope-every-day power. Because the room we were in was totally dark, it was impossible to determine when exactly the basket was lowered, yet it was always while I was sleeping, and the fare seldom varied: high fiber biscuits, veal broth and ripe olives for me, and carrots and oats for Dominique. These I would find waiting on top the heavy wooden dining table when I woke, and after emptying the bucket, I would replace the food basket with a metal pail that contained Dominique's and my own waste products. These also would be taken up again through the hole in the ceiling when I was asleep. Then I would sit with Dominique, say grace, and together we would eat. After we had finished, I would lay my head down on the wooden table and begin to dream.

This was the first step in my mantra of sleep, and nine out of ten times it worked. The second step was when Dominique and I somehow were released from our prison — why I was never certain — but I thought it might have been that our jailer, having realized he had imprisoned two humble and hardworking souls for so long, had chosen, rather than deny his mistake or even apologize, to merely rectify it instead, and return us to the world. In any case, it was only after our eyes adjusted to the light that I found our prison had been in fact a basement, with a roof made of tar paper, a small hole cut in its exact center, through which the food had been lowered. So we emerged, in this second stage, so to speak, with me leading Dominique, but both of us so weakened by a diet lacking in essential minerals, and wobbly enough from our lack of exercise to stagger around and bump into things in a fashion, I imagined, that had anyone been watching would be almost comical.

Then, when we at last had recovered our "land legs" so to speak, I climbed up on her back, and Dominique began to run, her neck outstretched for the first time in months, the streamers I had woven into her mane during my spare time trailing behind like the tail of a comet. They were crooked, of course, because I had to work in the dark, but there were *a lot* of them and in many colors. On all sides of us, Dominique and me, the Great Volume of the Prairie lay wide open for our inspection once again, with its "A" for fields of wild alfalfa, its "B" for buffalo, and its "C" for coiled rattlers, which Dominique smashed with her hoofs into reptile ellipses, commas, and semicolons.

So miles and miles the two of us traveled, in no particular direction, enchanted as we were with our suddenly renewed possibilities for choice. Each day we rode on, Dominique and I traversing a different page of the prairie's book, yet somehow reading and rereading the same text, searching in vain for a clue as to where we were heading. On some mornings, as I untangled myself from Dominique's bridle, the sun was on one side of me, and on others, it would be on the other. At times the two of us would meet strangers, fellow men and women, and horses, too (note opportunity for comic flirtations of animals mirroring the ways of human society), but mostly we remained mute wanderers who, if we spoke at all, chose to keep matters to a minimum.

Scene: A small campfire with Dominique and me and strangers and their horses.

Stranger: Care for some of my homemade buckwheat pancakes?

Me: No, thank you.

Stranger: Well, how about some escargot?

Me: Do you mean by that snails, Mister?

Stranger: Yes. Try one, though. I think you'll be pleasantly surprised.

Me: I guess I'll pass. Would you two care for some Vienna sausages or soda crackers?

Stranger: That's very generous of you. Thanks. Yes, we would.

And then I rolled up in Dominique's bridle, and would fall asleep.

Finally, if the previous scenario failed, as it did on the night I am in fact describing, my second back in my old house, there was one last shot. Dominique and I would wake the next morning, happy to share our breakfast with the company of friendly strangers, who provided a sort of buffet of bacon, sourdough rolls, coffee, cabbage and the beans left over from the night before.

Leader of the strangers: Say, I don't suppose you two would like to ride along with us.

Me: No, I guess we're not the following kind.

And so we leave, riding (well, I'm riding) across the prairie through dry washes and swift moving rivers which appear out of nowhere, sometimes travelling east, sometimes west, sometimes in circles, until at the end of the day we find the only tree around for miles, which we camp beneath. Shortly after supper, we are set upon by wolves, and though I am able to climb the tree to save myself from the ravenous beasts, clearly Dominique cannot, and I am forced to spend the night listening to her wild cries (mercifully short) but then the snarling, gulping, gnashing, and gnawing of the wolves, until by morning they leave, so in that awful dawn's first light, the only things left that I can recognize are Dominique's tail and her mane, still braided with a few pathetic, bloody streamers.

Me: Good-night, old friend. I'll remember you always.

Exhausted from my ordeal, I fell asleep without fail.

It was from this last troubled slumber I was waked by a knocking on the door. I rubbed my eyes. Standing in front of me were two elderly men, both wearing ski vests and hats with flaps that, in the case of extreme cold, could be pulled down over their ears. Odd costumes, I thought, for the temperatures found in St. Nils, and I was taken by a momentary twinge of nostalgia for Iceland. Still, I paid their haberdashery no mind beyond that, and attributed the winter clothing to the rigors of their advanced age, it being a well-known fact that the older a person gets, the more they crave warmth.

"Hello," said the taller of the two. "My name is David, and this is my helper, Steve. We're with the local phone company, and we may seem surprisingly old for this kind of work, but we were recently hired under a new law forbidding discrimination of senior citizens. I know it's unusual for you to receive service so soon after you requested it, but we seniors have a 'can do' attitude, and unlike our younger colleagues, we're grateful just to have a job. We happened to be in the neighborhood, and, having finished our last job ahead of schedule, we had some extra time on our hands. You look as if you've been asleep. If that's the case, we apologize. However, if you wish, we can connect your phone this very minute."

The men, draped in tools and adorned with ropes and pouches, clearly seemed to be who they claimed, so I invited them in and started a pot of coffee. "I don't suppose you'd like to join me in a little breakfast," I offered. "I just happened to have some frozen cod cakes I can thaw if you'd care to try some."

They accepted my offer of the coffee, but declined the cod. "That seems like a sort of strange thing for an American to eat this early in the day," Steve said suspiciously.

I told them that though I had lived here, in this very house in fact, in the past, I had just returned from over seven years spent in Iceland. After a conversation in which they expressed their own love for travelling to foreign places in general, but not necessarily Iceland in particular, they installed the phone. Then they returned for more coffee, during which time they told me about their own lives, which, because each of the men was pretty old, included a lot of events, particularly in David's case. Before he decided to retire, David had been an installer of wiretaps all over the world for the U. S. government. Quitting had been a mistake, David said, and he missed the respect he had been given by more poorly paid foreign operatives and their needy families.

For months, David said, after leaving government service he'd done nothing but mope around and play bingo, which had eaten up a surprising portion of his retirement savings. Finally the phone company had hired him. Then he closed with a harrowing description of a basement that he had run wires through only yesterday. It had been dark and covered with spider webs. "As old as I am, they still give me the creeps." He laughed apologetically, then looked over his shoulder at nothing in particular.

When their coffee was gone, the two senior citizens put away their cups. "Well, that's about it," they said, and they left, walking slowly back to their truck.

At last I was able to dial Emily's number once again. I hadn't wanted to trust the specialness of the moment to a pay phone, with its operators breaking through for more money and the irritating roar of traffic in the background. Finally, I reflected, I would be able hear her voice, and listen to her breath once again, and maybe, if everything was very quiet when she picked up the receiver, I would be able to detect the actual beat of her heart when, surprised by hearing my voice after all these years, she would press it to her breast for a moment to gain control of her emotions. But not so surprisingly, there was no answer at all, only a recorded voice, and nothing like the way I remembered Emily's own voice sounding.

"The number you have dialed is no longer in service," it said.

So it was that the second call I made was to the person I had actually intended to call in the first place, Dr. Pearlman. The doctor was not in, but his receptionist remembered me quite well, and she told me that she was amazed I was still alive. Since I had been a patient, she said, the doctor had unearthed four other cases of for-sure orgagenic disintegration, and one possible, but all five of them had expired. "I'm sure the doctor will be very interested in seeing you again at the first available opportunity so he can try to figure out how you've made it this far. Unfortunately he's booked for the next two months, so it will have to be after that. If there's an opening before then, I'll let you know."

I thanked her, made an appointment and hung up. Outside, I could see Dave and Steve still sitting in their truck, and could hear sporadic shouting. Apparently they had gotten into some altercation over their respective health-care plans. Those seniors might have a "can-do" attitude, but surely it came with a downside, too. I lay down on my couch to try to sort things out. I would pay a visit to the organ pool the next day, I decided. Then, exhausted by everything that had happened, I fell back to sleep.

The next morning I woke, somewhat chagrined to find that I'd fallen back into my old habit of cabbage for breakfast. I realized I must have been more worried than I'd thought.

After tidying up the dishes, I boarded the bus to the formerly elegant, and now beginning to be shabby, section of town where the organ pool was still located. Though I had feared it might have gone out of business in the seven years I'd been gone, the bus driver assured me that not only was it still there, but after a brief period of notoriety when it was attacked by a fundamentalist organization that had declared organ transplants to be the moral equivalent to wife swapping, it was doing a booming business. "It was on three different network news investigations, but you never know," he said, and winked. "All that publicity may even have helped."

Indeed, the grounds were well kept, and the exterior looked so prosperous that even before I entered the building I was filled with hopes of finding Emily, possibly promoted to some executive position by then. There was the same triangular frieze (I saw this time around that it was of a funeral procession), and the dark granite of the building's walls were surprisingly free of the sprays of neighborhood gangs announcing their territory.

"Emily," I shouted into the moist air, unable to contain myself, even before I'd passed through the front doors, "are you here?" But the sound of my voice only echoed emptily against the pink marbled interior. I stopped and looked around. There were the same statues of naughty nymphs and suggestive satyrs, but passing through the doors to the pool I discovered that what had been a single, Olympic-sized pool full of healthy organs was now divided, much as the cinemas of my childhood had also been, into four mini-pools.

Not only that, but in place of the beautiful woman who had so occupied my thoughts for the past seven plus years, instead there were groups of ancient men and women in baggy swim clothes and plastic bathing caps. They were, as nearly as I could tell, just standing in water up to their necks, moving their arms and bobbing up off the bottom like sodden corks. One of them, a wrinkled string bean of a blond who introduced herself as Betsy, called me over, and as I hunkered down at water's edge she filled me in on the changes that had taken place since I'd been there last.

Betsy explained that a few years ago the group of doctors responsible for the original organ idea were bought out by a multinational corporation, which had divided the single pool into four smaller ones, each with slight variations on the nutrients provided, depending on the body parts' special needs. But instead of having to hire three more scantily clad female attendants to accommodate the new arrangement, some genius in management figured out that they could rent all four of the pools to groups of arthritic senior citizens, the so-called Twinges-in-the-Hinges set. Thus, the organs received the same attention they were used to, and the pools actually turned a larger profit.

"Yes," Betsy mused, as meanwhile I watched the saline drying in Anacin-sized chunks on her leathery skin, "who ever would have dreamed that a low-impact exercise program in heated salt water, where the movements are gentle enough to have a healthy effect on joints, would be the exact motion required to stimulate delicate organs? And in addition," she added with a sparkle in her eye, "there's also the generally unspoken bonus that we have a chance to meet the organ we may well own in the future." Then, rather inappropriately, I thought, Betsy invited me in to join her and her friends. I left, disheartened, and walked back to give myself more time to think. It seemed that Emily's trail was getting cold, and so after lunch (still more cabbage!) I took a stroll to the local library, where I checked out the obituaries, and belatedly realized two important things. First, that I never knew Emily's last name, so there was not much point to that particular exercise, and second, that the very name "Emily" itself might well have been a *nom de plume,* one she had given out on a sort of trial basis while she was deciding whether or not she wanted to take the first tentative steps to an enduring relationship.

Reeling with the weight of that realization, I sat in my

straight-backed chair, and quietly inhaled the book dust. An elderly gentleman who shared his table panted pleasantly, as if he were a dog and this was a hot day (which it was not), over an art book of nudes. My mind drifted. Suddenly, the panting brought me back to another time and place when Emily herself, lying on her back, had been panting slightly. For that matter, I also had been panting a bit as I stared down at a single ant strolling obliviously along a line of grout.

"Look at that ant down there," I'd said. "Don't you suppose that he believes he's the center of his world the same as you and me? Don't you suppose that he has his own joys and sorrows, disappointments and triumphs, just like us?"

Emily stared at the insect for a moment, then reached down and pressed her finger firmly down to crush it. "Sure," she said, "but sometimes doesn't all of this just seem futile?" Then she stared for a moment at a passing cloud that looked remarkably like a retractable ballpoint pen.

"I mean," Emily continued, "what's the difference, and I mean no slight by this, between the orgasm I just experienced with you a few seconds ago and the one that preceded it? Don't mistake me: They were both pleasant, and must have been different, of course. Yet right now, only seconds after the last and minutes after the first, I would be hard pressed to describe the particulars of how this was so."

Then Emily panted a bit more. "For that matter," she explained, "after the first breath we take, how do all the others differ? Once again, they must, but if one is unable to say *how*, what is the point of thinking they are different? And if nothing differs, why bother going on to the next day? I mean, don't *you* ever just want to be free from this vast veil of desire and illusion? Don't you ever want to retract this whole silly business that assumes, without a single other example to measure it against, the *a priori* importance of human life?"

"Whoa," I'd said, "where does that kind of talk come from?"

But now, sitting in the library, having recently read her letter, of course I knew, or at least had a good idea. Next to me the rate of the old man's panting increased, and he began to rock ever-so-slightly in his chair. I walked briskly back home.

Time passed. Days, even weeks went by. Then eventually another patient canceled his appointment and Dr. Pearlman was able to find the time to see me four days early. Despite what his receptionist had told me, it was only halfway through my exam, a series of complicated tests and probings, that Dr. Pearlman appeared to remember he had treated me once, years ago.

"Oh yes," he said, "I've been having terrible trouble with my memory lately, and I'm afraid it may be something in my diet. You were my very first case of orgagenic disintegration, and I'm sorry to say at this stage it appears that your organ is completely beyond the stage of replacement." Then, seeing my startled expression, he went on.

"Think of the New York Stock Exchange," he said. "The organ in question has by now set up such a complex system of responses-to and contracts-with the other stock offerings of your body that even to interrupt its unsatisfactory functioning for a few minutes would be enough to send the Dow Jones, by which I mean any so-called healthy organ that remains, into such absolute distress, that the Big Board itself, by which I mean you, would surely fail."

For once I did not panic, but instead used this time to study Dr. Pearlman for clues as to the seriousness of my condition. It was a good sign, I thought, that as he spoke his pudgy hands remained clasped and rested on a brown blotter. As he stared through his gold-rimmed glasses straight into my eyes, I could see the reflection of a fluorescent light on a bald part of the man's skull. If he were worried, I thought, he would avoid my gaze all together. Yes, I thought, if an artist were commissioned to paint a picture, the purpose of which was to evoke calmness and expertise, it would be none other than Dr. Pearlman. Surely if there were anything seriously wrong, the doctor would not stay so calm. Surely he would be affected by the news of my organ's redisintegration as much as I was. Surely Dr. Pearlman would be far more agitated. His glasses would be askew. He would sweat. His breath would be shallow. Just like the guy in the library, he would begin to pant, and he would not look like an actor in his white doctor's smock, sitting in front of his shelf of gilt-titled medical books, checking his watch to see if it was time to go for lunch. Surely, I thought, as I caught a glimpse of my own self in the mirror, sweat rolling off me as off a football in the rain, he would look more like me.

"But on the other hand," Dr. Pearlman continued, preparing to insert yet another metaphor into the conversation, "like one of those cars one sometimes sees on the evening news, balancing half-on and half-off a cliff, the panicked occupant inside staring out, afraid to move lest he tip the balance, signaling frantically for help, there's no telling exactly how long you might last. It's even possible this new arrangement your organs have come up with might turn out to be superior to the original one, just as the invention of margarine, with its lower cho-

138

lesterol and superior spreadability, has gradually come to replace butter in the minds of most healthy individuals, which,
by the way, you are not one of. Did I mention that all my other
patients with your disorder have long since died? Well, think
positive. The good news here is that you haven't."

I thanked him and left, not forgetting to give a farewell
wave to the receptionist on the way out.

Walking back from the doctor's office (Iceland had made
a walker out of me, it seemed) I thought about how time changes
things. The street signs and buildings I was passing, for example, were mostly the same ones I remembered from seven
years ago, when I had first needed an organ transplant. Back
then I had a sick organ, and I had one again, but apparently
seven years later my organ was a different kind of sick. Or was
it the same sick organ, but now the other organs around it had
changed? Had those buildings and street signs in fact been al-
tered in my absence? They *must* have been, so in fact my
memory must have graciously accommodated the changes into
its picture of the past. Even the Treasure Chest sign, as bright
as I remembered it seven years earlier, must surely have been
repainted at one time or another, so was it the same sign, or a
different one? All this thinking was giving me a headache, and
all I wanted was to get indoors, into a dark room, to pour myself a glass of distilled water, and to pop a few aspirins. But
when I arrived outside my old/new house whom did I see, out
in front, but of all people, the phone men, Dave and Steve, still
wearing the exact same (or were they?) heavy, quilted jackets
and caps they had worn on their previous visit. They were doing something up on the pole by the corner, but I couldn't tell
what.

For a moment I toyed with the idea of just walking on down the street, maybe even paying a visit to the bookstore, and returning when they'd left, but my headache was too painful. I had to get indoors, so I passed by them, pretending they weren't there, took the aspirins, put a cool towel over my forehead, and shut my eyes for about twenty minutes. When my headache receded a bit, I ambled outside.

"Hey! You guys!" I called from the front door. "Do you have time for a cup of coffee?"

But instead of answering, they hastily climbed into their van, and drove off, doubtless to another installation.

So quickly did the two depart that I began to wonder if I had actually seen them. It was possible they weren't even real, but some sort of afterimage from my previous sighting, possibly brought on by the pain in my head. But if I had imagined them, or if they actually were there, then what was the difference? Were they really Dave and Steve? How could I be sure? Though I hated to admit it, the same might have also been true for Emily herself. I knew that I hadn't seen her in years, but her presence still remained, didn't it? Well, didn't it? I stared out the window at the place where Dave and Steve may or may not have recently stood, and then it came to me, as it probably had come to countless others: What actually had happened was less important than what I believed had happened, or believed hadn't happened, for that matter, because that was also a kind of belief.

I remembered reading an article during my recent visit to Dr. Pearlman's office that detailed the effects of Cretzfeldt-Jakob Disease, complete with illustrations. It explained how over years a patient's brain fills up with masses of fibrous cells, a conglomeration it humorously compared to Spackle, and it suddenly came to me that philosophy was like that. The germ I'd picked up from Emily, which had remained mostly dormant during my Icelandic years, had returned in full force.

The only thing I could think of to combat this inward tendency was action. I had to find Emily again, no matter what, and somehow, returning to this same house where I'd heard her first message on my phone machine had brought that all back. I had no phone machine at that moment, and made plans to go out and buy one soon, but how would Emily be able to leave a message after its tone, when thus far the conventional wisdom of patience and a little research had failed?

I had to try something, but what? I had to turn somewhere, but where? I was desperate, and I promise here once and for all that I would not have done what I did next had there been any possibility other than this single, ridiculous, childish gesture, no matter how unpromising, I promise I would have tried it. But instead what I did was this: I pulled down the window shades, shut my eyes, and walked to the middle of the room. Then I unzipped my trousers, and grasped my penis firmly in my right hand. (This really is *so* embarrassing — and it's only the fact that you have already been through two complete physical exams with me so far that I can hope you won't be offended.)

Next, as if I was holding the needle of a compass, I began to turn around slowly, waiting for some sensation, however faint, that might direct me to Emily. I turned once, twice, three times, and . . . Bingo! Got a bite! When I opened my eyes I was pointing north. It occurred to me that I might have been unduly influenced by my metaphor. Once again I shut my eyes, and replacing the compass idea with that of a dowser's rod, I began to turn around once again, more slowly this time. Once again I waited for the twinge that would point me to Emily.

I turned around and around, and just as I was getting dizzy, I thought I felt something. It turned out to be just a piece of skin caught in my zipper. I revolved again, more carefully. Then all at once it was present: an unmistakable tug by a force greater than me. I opened my eyes to find I was facing the sweating ceramic watercooler, and hanging above it was a painting of a man, seemingly in prayer. I studied it more closely. The man was middle-aged and slightly bald, and the expression on his face was remarkably serene, as if whatever doubts the man might have had about the value of his own life, whatever qualms or trepidation he might have felt about choosing between a life of action or one of contemplation, they had at last all been resolved. I returned my penis to my underwear, its job completed, and cautiously zipped back up. The painting had been there since I moved in, of course; it was one of the furnishings still left back from the days before I had gone to Iceland, so long ago, but had I ever really *looked* at it? I stepped closer and turned on the floor lamp, tilting its shade upward so the light shined directly on its surface. Clearly the answer to the last question was a resounding "no."

The man was not praying at all, but instead attempting to clean a rather large stain from the rug on which he knelt, and what I had mistaken for a robe of some sort was actually a large pair of overalls. Nor was the rug itself one of those commonplace floor coverings made of the sort of uniform pastel polyester mostly designed to conceal dirt that is found in so many modern homes. No, this rug clearly had been woven by hand, and depicted a scene that, dirty or clean, was striking in its own right. The pattern on the rug showed a watery expanse, lit only by a moon, with glints of light striking the surface of the water (it was clearly a lake or an ocean, because no land was in sight) on which bobbed (if objects in a still picture could be said to bob) a large ship (although there was nothing next to it to compare it with), along with various other items of different size and shapes (generally having in common the traits of darkness and a certain roundness to their corners, like those bags of trash reputed to be thrown off the decks of luxury liners when the crew believes its passengers are fast asleep).

Above the surface of the sea (if it was really a sea) there were a few dramatic clouds, but other than those clouds and a solitary bird, maybe an albatross or fish hawk, the sky was eerily empty. Weirdly though, beneath the surface of the water, a light shined, as if a volcano was in the process of erupting, and by its faint glow the viewer could perceive that the sea, unlike the mostly sterile air, was teeming with life. Beneath the soggy carpet of kelp and jellyfish that floated on its surface I could make out the silhouettes of sleek salmon searching blindly for their streams, sharks, flounder, halibut, lobsters, scallops, Dover sole, red snapper, octopus, squid, eels, swordfish, mahi-mahi, cod, crab, striped bass, calico bass, sea bass, mackerel, ocean perch and sardines, tuna, haddock, bonita, and yellowtail. In addition, there were the foggy, majestic forms of sea turtles, the near blind but no less majestic forms of seals and whales, and the completely blind and not at all majestic forms of sea cucumbers, oysters, and clams. Amidst them floated clouds of krill and forests of seaweed, some towering two and three hundred feet high, rich in protein and iodine, a resource for the world's hungry, only barely tapped into at the moment I stood there, viewing the picture.

I began to get dizzy again. What *was* the message for me, exactly? Certainly, familiar themes were within my reach, but just how familiar they were, and how they might aid me in my quest for Emily was unclear. I stared, and thought, and thought some more. What was the meaning of all of this? And then, at last it came to me. It was just possible the clue my penis had been directing me to with such insistence did not lie in the pattern of the unusual rug itself, but elsewhere in the picture, somewhere in the rest of the room where the rug had been spread out. Accordingly, I turned my revived attention to the details I had initially overlooked.

The first thing that caught my eye in this regard was a largish object standing in one corner of the room. It was a piano, an old one of the upright variety, with chipped and yellowed keys very like the one I myself used to practice upon as a boy when I had finished mending fences and feeding Dominique. A square of white sheet music, which, judging by the black marks that indicated notes, was an étude by Chopin (one of my own favorite pieces), had been left out, as if the pianist had been perhaps playing, and then, disturbed by the heavyset man kneeling on the rug, had left, planning to return to his demanding but heavenly music when the man finished cleaning the rug. Or, I supposed, it was also possible that the heavyset man himself had been the pianist, and something, maybe one of his contact lenses, had fallen onto the floor.

In the opposite corner from the piano was a sofa, oddly covered in a garish plaid very like the sofa my own parents had kept in the recreation room at our ranch, and upon which I had first experienced the terror and uncertainty of my first teen-age forays into the world of sex and adulthood with a sweet girl who lived on the ranch next door, and who later became a smoke-jumper, I was told. Next to the picture's sofa was an end table, the curved legs of which held a small brass lamp, rather like the one my parents had in their bedroom when I was a child. Its light was on, and lying on the end table was an open medical dictionary, turned (I could just barely make it out) to an entry that looked to be "Organs."

Finally, midway between the piano and the end table with the lamp there was the half-illuminated skeleton of a birdcage, and behind its shadowy bars, a small dot of yellow that I guessed might be a canary. I stared at the painting before me, like an ape before a cathedral, trying to puzzle out what it might mean. Was it possible that Emily, represented here by the canary, was being held prisoner somewhere? But where? I assembled and disassembled its elements as if it were a typewriter designed to reproduce the alphabet of an alien race. Finally, I came up with the solution. The only possible meaning of this particular com-bination was a piano bar by the sea. And truthfully, though it didn't seem much to go on, it was the only thing that made sense. Besides, what did I have to lose?

I took the picture down from the wall. Behind it was a spot where a large chunk of plaster had apparently fallen out, most likely the reason the painting had been hung there in the first place. I turned the painting over. On its back was a note, the letters of which were nearly vertical, occasionally sloping to the left or to the right as waves of security or insecurity flowed through the writer's body into his or her hands and straight down to the moving pen. "See you soon . . . E." As short as the sentence was, certain letters, I noticed, were identical, the *N* and the *U*, for example, and also that the word *soon*, was broken in three places. Plus, there were enough sharp angles and corners to make the conclusion inescapable that the writer, whoever she (or, I had to add for the sake of scientific impartiality, "he") was, was clearly in pain. I found the letter from Emily had sent seven years ago and studied it. I couldn't be sure, but the handwriting could have been the same. And the ink was the same, faded brown.

I thought about it: a piano bar by the sea. After all, how many places like that could actually exist? A dozen at most, was my guess. How hard would it be to take a few driving lessons, learn to drive, get a license, rent a car, buy a little insurance, and then cruise a few communities up and down the coast from St. Nils? Then I would visit their watering holes, and find Emily in one of them, a little angry after waiting all this time for a reply to her letter, but I imagined, on the whole, glad to see me. My answer was that it would not be very hard at all, but before I began such an undertaking, it might be a good idea to start with the environs of St. Nils itself, by foot and by bus.

The first thing I learned, much to my surprise, was that to define exactly what made a piano bar a piano bar was no piece of cake. For example, though it was clearly easy to eliminate those bars which had no actual piano, and simple also to cross off the odd piano lacking a bar, one of the discouraging discoveries I made was that, for one reason or another, many bars still had operative pianos, and from time to time people still dropped by to use them. But even eliminating amateur use, I ran into another problem. Namely, that while a bar might have hired a player the previous week, and might again the following week, on the actual day of my visit none would be present. So did that count or not? Some places, I noted, had piano players on Fridays and Saturdays, while still others had them on Sundays, Mondays and Tuesdays, or Mondays, Wednesdays, and Fridays. In other words, when I stopped to tally them this way the number of potential piano bars soared quickly into the hundreds. Or was this mode of thinking just a new and more deadly form of the philosophy virus? I couldn't be certain.

It soon became apparent that before I could eliminate any bar as a possibility, I would have to spend two or three months in any given area, going out night after night, eating salted peanuts, sipping cocktails, and listening to a parade of sad stories until each place shut down. And even then (although I chose not to dwell on this), how could I be sure that Emily wasn't walking by outside on her way to another bar right down the street the very minute I was sitting in my own establishment, sipping, say, a Cock o' the Walk, or a Bloody Russian? Or, for that matter, even if I had managed to get the right bar, hers, suppose Emily had taken a night off from drinking to do her laundry, or go to the library, or watch an old movie on TV? Could she do all this while being held prisoner? I didn't know, but perhaps her jailer was none other than her addiction. All in all it was a frustrating and grueling business, and had I known at the beginning what I was about to get myself into, I doubt I ever would have begun.

Thus it happened that I had already visited The Boathouse (near the Marina), The Whirlpool Lounge (overlooking the ocean), The Psyclops Room (a watering hole for the staff of a nearby state mental hospital), and the Don't Come Inn (a meeting spot for private investigators, none of whom were of any help to me), before I arrived at the Calypso Bar and Grill, where I became sidetracked for quite a while.

The Calypso, as the name implies, was a Caribbean-themed bar. It was located in a sort of windowless step-down from a pet shop, and its entrance was predictably plastered over with red and blue fake rocks to form a grotto, its front door adorned with a porthole formed out of heavy rope. The Calypso catered, to my not-so-great surprise, to those patrons wishing for a taste of the carefree life of the Caribbean. In other words, not so much to any former native who, having fled its grinding poverty and boot-licking tourist-driven economy, might be so nostalgic for his native land as to accept this ersatz substitute, as to those former tourists who had once vacationed in that lovely area of the world and just couldn't let go of a good time. And while, judging by the picture over the bar, the Calypso in its more prosperous days had live palm trees and a real steel band, by the time I arrived, economic hard times had long since struck and stayed. Those palms of long ago had been replaced by a single one made from unpleasantly green plastic, and the former four-piece band by a lone piano player. True, the place still served its tall tropical punches, strong rums and wallop-packing Cokes, but as time had passed, the number of the clientele seemed to have frozen at about fifteen, and even that modest number was in danger of diminishing, as one by one the bar's aging customers sailed back to that other bar, on death's own mainland.

The first evening I arrived, things were, I have to say, slow. The limbo stick was covered with dust, and when the bar's patrons joined in for the chorus of "The Banana Boat Song" their voices were cracked and feeble. Not only that, but when they came to the words, "Come Mister Tally Man, tally me banana," the words "Tally Man" suddenly assumed a dark and ominous quality, while the phrase "daylight come and me want to go home" took on a quality of infinite longing and resignation. Nor was it uncommon, I learned in later visits, as the last words of the song ended, to find three or four of the patrons quietly sobbing into their Coco-locos.

Was this Emily's kind of bar? I scarcely knew her, but I thought probably not. So why did I stay so long at the Calypso? At first I told myself "just to be sure," but in retrospect, I suppose it was that anyone at all who walked into the Calypso for the first time was made to feel unbelievably welcome, and I certainly had the need for company. In those first few days as I waited for Emily to appear I became the recipient of who-knows-how-many Zombies and Rum Punches pressed into my hands by other patrons, and in the process, I soon learned that there was more to the Calypso than free drinks, a run-down atmosphere, and an undeniable taste of bathos. Camaraderie aside, I have to admit what really kept me at the Calypso for the six years or so that followed my first walk through its door (all those mixed drinks have left me a little vague when it comes to measuring the passage of time) was not so much my fellow celebrants, but rather the presence of the bartender herself, Calypso Sally.

And although yes indeed, there *was* something touching and brave about those hardy souls who partied night after night as if to distract themselves from the stern gaze of their own mortality, they were not the ones who caught me so off guard that very first slightly rainy evening I arrived. Instead it was Sally herself, as the piano player swung into what was apparently a tradition of the place, a rendition of a song he had composed in honor of the place's mistress:

> Calypso Sally! She got to be so fine!
> She mix that rum and pour that wine:
> Chablis, sauterne, and cabernet;
> She take you down to Frenchman Bay!

I turned to watch what Sally would do during this presentation, and much to my surprise, instead of the happy, resigned smile I had expected as a matter of course in such circumstances, Sally blushed a deep and enduring red. Then her eyes filled with thick tears, which she blinked back. Why had none of the other patrons noticed this, or were their coarser gazes too busy consuming the luscious curves of her body, the plunging line of her bodice, the delicate wings of her collar bones and the miracle of her tiny ears, each not much larger than a quarter? Could I have been wrong? Was it some new mutation of the philosophy virus? It was possible, I thought. But it was also possible I'd been mistaken, that maybe Calypso Sally had a speck of dust, or a beautiful lash lodged in her beautiful eye. Just to be sure I returned a second night, and a third as well. On all of them, at about 11:30, when the room filled with the patrons' shouts for "Calypso Sally," and the piano player obligingly began its easy rhythms, I watched her again to see if I was correct.

And I was. Not just the first time, but also the second and the third as well, she blushed, and her eyes brimmed up with blinked-back tears, as she bit her lip. Then she would turn away for a minute, pretending to check the level on a bottle of vodka or to count the lemon peels, returning to her customers only after she had regained her self-control. Afterwards, with a radiantly false smile, she offered the entire bar a free round of drinks.

So time passed, and then even more time, and I became a regular, the Calypso in a way my second home. But it was only later, on an evening where it was clear I was in no condition to drive back to my real home that Sally took me to hers, and I learned the story behind her sadness. Sally lived in an apartment, an old brick building that smelled of mock orange, in a part of St. Nils that was actually called Frenchman's Bay. Inside were 1) a gray covered ironing board permanently left out, 2) thick red curtains on the windows, 3) a hot plate, 4) a refrigerator humming in the corner, and 5) a complete set of the Modern Library Editions, read and annotated.

"I've always loved books," Sally said with a self-deprecating gesture. "When I gave up my career as a classical pianist, they became my comfort and support as well. As a pianist, I specialized in Chopin, and according to my teachers, I was supposed to be the next Rubenstein. I don't really know if they were right or not, though, because of one thing: I had stage fright so bad I had to stop appearing in public, and couldn't even dream of taking part in any competitions. You may have noticed at the bar how I hate being looked at. But even that wouldn't have been so bad, if it were just the usual kind of aversion, the kind that comes and goes, and you learn to get over it, but that wasn't my story.

"There I'd be, playing some waltz or étude, whatever, feeling fine, lost in the beauty of the phrasing and all those great notes, when something would click inside my head, and I'd realize how pretentious the very idea of playing was. And not just playing, but doing anything at all memorable. How laughable I was, it would seem to me, to even attempt to leap out of the muted carpet of world history, the floor covering that includes in its threads the extinction of whole species, the movement of continents and the pummeling of the earth by asteroids. Who was I compared to all others who had gone before and would come after? I was a joke; an object of derision. Then I would freeze."

"My God," I thought. "The Philosophy Virus . . ." but Sally continued:

"At first, my parents sent me to a specialist, and I began to improve; sometimes I would finish an étude clear to the end, and at others I would stop, although in general I felt that things were getting better. But then, things took a turn for the worse. That is, when word of my condition got out, certain music critics and fellow musicians went so far as to place bets, some of them quite substantial, over which spot in the composition, during which movement or bar, I would lapse into silence, staring dumbly my piano.

"It was horrible. If I played well, if I got through two or three or even four concerts without a mishap, the size of the bets kept going up, like the lottery. Then, when I finished the concert, instead of supportive cheers I deserved because I had overcome a major handicap, or even played well, God forbid, instead I would hear the boos of disappointed bettors. If, on the other hand, I suddenly froze, sat glued mutely to the piano bench, looking down the abyss of my own vanity and foolish expectations, some lucky idiot was sure to start cheering.

"So I quit. You'll notice that there is no music in this apartment," Sally said. All at once I realized that this was true. I swallowed hard. I had never known a classical pianist, and to imagine one running a piano bar, having to hear those catchy, inane melodies night after night . . . it seemed practically too much, but Sally continued:

"The Calypso, the drinks, the smell of alcohol, the gradual diminishment of the patrons, the clouds of smoke — I find all of them, except for the simple-hearted rhythms of the West Indies, to be nearly intolerable. Strangely, I have to say there's something about the sheer unpretentiousness of the songs and innocence of the lyrics that makes them the exception to my rule, because, you see, I still love music. So, a few years ago, when my parents died in a freak automobile accident, I took my modest inheritance, and bought the Calypso, where, over the last ten years, my sole creative act has been the invention of my own personal alcoholic cocktail, 'The Volcano,' a mixture of vodka, tabasco, cassis (for color), vinegar and baking soda. It was a runner-up two years ago at the State Bartender Mixed Drink Derby, and should be served in an inverted funnel with a straw, so the drinker can finish off their beverage once the volcanic action has died down." Then she blushed.

And it was at that exact moment, I believe, that I fell in love with Calypso Sally.

Not that I can't imagine what you are thinking, because, in a way, I've already thought it myself. You are thinking, "What is it with this guy? I can understand how he could go from Emily to Greta, particularly because Greta looked almost exactly like Emily, but in reverse, and together they shared a life-and-death situation, but come on, how sincere can his attachment for Emily have been if no sooner had he embarked on his search for the woman of his dreams than he stopped, as if he were some so-called pioneer on his way to California, maybe even St. Nils, and never got farther than Ohio?"

To which I have two answers: First, if you had been reading closely you would have noticed that I did spend a lot of time in the Calypso before I actually fell in love, and second, that I'm a little embarrassed too — except that when I looked into Sally's deep and sincere brown eyes (and you will note she resembled neither Emily nor Greta) that I only wanted to hold her in my arms and defend her from all the jeers and laughter that this, or any other, world could dish out. "Oh yeah?" I wanted to say. "You think you're so tough, picking on a classical pianist. . . . Well, what do you say to a typewriter repairman? Take that! And that!"

But that, in a way, was precisely the problem: Namely, that my Sally, beautiful and shy, with her long pianist's fingers, her chestnut brown hair, and her sensitivity had already begun the process of protecting herself by taking large quantities of drugs, and in the process acquired a serious habit. And thus, like all star-crossed lovers, our crossing — that is, Sally's and mine — was laid out from the very beginning. On the one hand it was obvious from the start that Sally was far too beautiful to be left alone at the bar as she had been when I first walked in, but on the other hand, who among her customers wanted to hang out for drinks, watching some beautiful chick and her boyfriend? Very few, that's who. And so when word got out that she and I were an item, business dropped off a cliff, and with it, the profits from the bar. Not only that, just about that time I was scraping out the bottom of the sack that contained the last proceeds from my sale of the typewriter repair business to Snori, and the last of my insurance money from the ava-lanche settlement. I never told her about that last part, though.

Sally took this turn of events, as she did nearly every-thing, gracefully, and even tried to save money at first by cut-ting back on the amount of the drugs she used. Little by little she watered them down with cornstarch and talcum powder, until at last, she attempted to do without them altogether. For a short time it worked. Night after night, after the closing of the bar, I would read aloud to Sally from the Modern Library Edition of *Crime and Punishment,* while holding her head in my hands, watching the soft brown hair at the base of her neck grow damp with perspiration as she vomited into the toilet bowl (which I took pride in making as clean as possible).

"Oh, honey," she would say. "It hurts so bad."

Often a small string of bile would accompany these whis-pered words, and I could tell that it had hurt her to talk at all. Then I would wipe her face with a damp face towel.

"Honey, honey, please," Sally said, and I held her hand and supported her in going "cold turkey" for as long as I could. But how long could that be when the woman I loved was suf-fering and my own money was gone? What kind of person would I be if I saw this and did nothing? Finally, I did the only thing I could think of: I made up my mind to rob a conve-nience store, or several, if that's what it took, and to use the proceeds from my crime, or crimes, to help support Sally's habit. The following day, with surprisingly little difficulty I purchased a pistol from one of the bar's regulars, a retired cop, and em-barked, full of optimism, on my new career.

The first several convenience stick-ups (I enjoyed calling them that — it made them sound like a generic brand of room deodorizer) went smoothly. I would stroll in, my head covered by an ordinary brown paper bag with two holes cut out for eyes and one for the mouth. Then I would notice the usually bored expressions on the clerks' faces change to amusement, then to alertness as I waved the gun and shouted, "This is a stick-up!" The only really unexpected bonus was how often the clerks, underpaid and viciously exploited by their bosses, seemed glad for a little excitement, as often as not yelling after me, "Be sure to take a six-pack!"

And so I got into the habit of leaving the bar about midnight on Tuesdays and Thursdays, our slowest nights, robbing a convenience store (occasionally two) and returning to the Calypso to help shut the doors and clean up. In time Sally reestablished her maintenance dosage and returned to the business of coping with a poor self-image and running a barely successful piano bar, and it may have been only my imagination, but it seemed to me that Sally was doing better. At the Treasure Chest one day I found an inexpensive keyboard, which I brought home and left lying in a conspicuous place. Late one night I came home from a robbery to find her quietly and thoughtfully picking out the notes to "Good King Wenceslas" (it was around Christmas) and when she saw me watching she blushed and turned away. Still, I was encouraged.

At the last place I chose to rob, however, things went wrong from the start. To begin with, I hadn't made the eyeholes for my bag large enough, so when I erroneously believed I heard a noise behind me and whirled around, gun in hand, I crashed into a CD rack containing bargain-priced hits of the fifties. In truth I should have just left at that point, because the clerk, whether out of annoyance at the mess I'd just created, or because he had to interrupt his reading from one of the several magazines the store carried on entrepreneurship, was not so compliant as others had been in the past.

"This is a stick-up," I said.

"Don't be silly," was the clerk's reply. "That sounds like a room deodorant. OK, I'll tell you what — let's split it."

"Ninety/Ten," I answered.

"Fifty-five/Forty-five," the counter-clerk countered, "or I'll blow your head off with the shotgun I've got hidden behind the counter."

He must have been reading an article on negotiation. Just my luck. "I don't believe you," I said. "Eighty-five/Fifteen, and not a nickel more."

"Sixty-five/Thirty-five," the clerk answered, "and that's my final offer. It's a twelve-gauge, semiautomatic, with a cut-down barrel, manufactured by the aptly named Savage Arms Company."

We settled at Seventy/Thirty, but unfortunately, just as the two of us had the contents of the cash register divided into two piles on the counter, with me still wearing the bag on my head, a patrolman came in to pick up a free cup of coffee and a skin magazine. At that precise moment the clerk lost his nerve.

"Help," he shouted, "a stick-up!"

Annoyed at the interruption, the cop pulled out his gun and pointed it at me. In short, I was handed a sentence of ten years, with time off for good behavior.

Thus it happened I entered a new and more rigorous stage of my life, one that while it was certainly necessary to go through in order to move on to the next (whatever happened to that "flow" business, anyway?), also would have been perfectly OK to have skipped. I had said a tearful goodbye to Sally, who herself had been taken off to a completely different pen for possession of the narcotics they'd found when they searched her apartment. As they dragged her out the door she'd whispered, "I am *so* bummed out for you, and I know you meant well, but really, I kind of wish we'd never met."

I felt terrible, of course, but those words of Sally's also had the ring of a judgement. *Had* I brought about her arrest? *Should* I have just minded my own business? Maybe, that's what prison was all about — a sort of lesson on how not to interfere. Then the next thing I knew I was being driven off to my new home, a formidable looking building of concrete and steel. Curiously, it was there, after my initial physical examination, that I received two pieces of good news.

The doctor, after he had finished washing his hands several times, told me in answer to my question, that my organ appeared to have healed itself during the years I had spent with Sally.

"As odd as it may be," the doctor, a tall man with a barely noticeable wen, said, "it seems that a steady diet of salted nuts and sickeningly sweet alcoholic beverages may be exactly what we in the medical community need to start prescribing for cases of orgagenic disintegration." Then he wished me good luck, and that was also the last I ever saw of him, too, because on the strength of the article he published about my condition in a minor medical journal, the man was hired at a considerable salary by a consortium of liquor distributors and peanut farmers.

The second piece of good news came several weeks later. Early one morning as I was being escorted out of "The Hole," as they called it, I heard a familiar sound. I should add that I hadn't done anything in particular to merit "The Hole," which was a dark, warm, smelly place, but was told that it was the policy of the warden that new arrivals receive a taste of what was in store for them if they misbehaved. In any case, walking back to my cell, which I had barely gotten a chance to finish decorating before they'd taken me off to "The Hole," I heard a sound behind a door, followed by much cursing.

"What's in there?" I asked the guard, who either because he was less hardened by prison life than some, or was grateful that I had not complained about my treatment, answered, "Oh, that's the room where you prisoners work on your appeals."

"And what do they use to write with?" I asked.

"Why, typewriters, of course," he said, incredulous that anyone could be so stupid.

And at that moment it was as if a portal had suddenly been blasted out of the hard concrete walls of the prison, a door, leading not to the cell where I would be spending most of my time for several years, but to the start of a new/old career.

For it turned out that in the hurly-burly of the technological revolution that had put me so completely out of business in the United States of America, one of the last sanctuaries of the old ways was none other than the prison system. Though it (the system) kept track of us, its inmates, our merits and demerits, through its sophisticated and sleek banks of computers, when it came time for us to appeal our convictions, the only tools it meted out were a phalanx of broken-down typewriters, and indeed, I think the warders would not have done even that except that a commission on prisoners' rights had appeared one day to complain to the governor.

But what machines they turned out to be, with sticky keys, bent hammers, gummy cartridges and inkless ribbons, the whole situation made undoubtedly worse by the fact that their users, for the most part individuals with particularly low frustration tolerances, would bang, hit, kick and throw them across the room when they did not perform. All this behavior, of course, with the tacit approval of the room's monitors.

"We told you these people needed to be locked up," they seemed to say. "We told you these people did not deserve even the most basic of human rights, the right to appeal these sentences. *Now* will you believe us?"

But it wasn't long before word got out that for a fee (actually a rather sizeable one) I could adjust, correct, align, one of these battered machines into a superb writing instrument. Not only was I able to command a fair price (for the first time in my life) to put the machines back in shape, but one day, quite by accident, a subsidiary operation of rentals also developed. The rate of corrections overturned and sentences reduced skyrocketed. Some of the state's most dangerous felons were walking the streets in nearly no time from the minute they were first brought in, thanks to a touch typing course I also offered on the side.

Of course, when the prison officials found out who was responsible for all of this they made my life difficult. They threw me back in "The Hole," where this time, using the techniques my old Dutch teacher had shown me, smuggled parts and a tablespoon, I repaired the broken typewriters and sent them back into the light of day again nearly as quickly as they arrived. Giving up on "The Hole" as a deterrent, the officials turned to threats, promising a string of violations that would add years to my sentence, until one of them realized that would merely prolong their problem, and so after serving only half my original sentence I found myself one foggy morning, a fifty dollar bill in hand, paroled back to the streets of St. Nils.

So I left the prison in a hurry (who wouldn't?) and headed back to Sally's. It was a long shot, I knew, having heard not a word from her over the past five years, but I hoped that Sally still somehow might be living there, might somehow have gotten out of jail herself. If she had, I saw no sign of it, alas. But a lot could happen in five years, and not surprisingly, her apartment building at Frenchman's Bay had been sold, and a clinic dispensing diet pills was located in the same spot where our love nest used to be.

Nor did I fare any better when I returned to the site of the Calypso Room itself. Upstairs, the pet shop was still operating, but in place of the tropical-themed bar where I had spent so many nights was a computer service center, its owner a quietly industrious Armenian who had never heard of a limbo stick, although rumors had reached him of Sally herself.

"I don't know," he said. "I hear she nice person. She friend of yours? She there; she meet bad guy, then police take them both away, like this . . ." and for emphasis he pushed "delete" on the keyboard in front of him.

Unsure where to turn next, I found myself making a depressingly familiar choice. I paid a visit to my former landlord, but although my old place was vacant, the man seemed to show little interest in having me back.

"No offense," he said, looking down over a pair of bifocals I hadn't remembered in the past, "but the place hasn't exactly been lucky for you, and the last time you left I found a huge mess of strange wires and electronic boxes attached to the phone lines beneath the house. It practically took a bomb squad to take them out, and your security deposit didn't cover half the cost. I've always liked you, and still do. But you're an ex-con and all. Maybe you should see if you could find some place, well, smaller."

I looked at him. He had aged a lot over the dozen or so years that separated my last visit from this one. Sometimes people went that way — changed all of a sudden — and for others, time moved more slowly. For me, for example, as many other guys in prison, I'd made good use of the weight room, and though I couldn't deny that I'd aged — my hair was starting to turn gray in places — I had to say I'd pretty much held my own.

All except for, possibly, my organ. Maybe it was my imagination, or maybe the absence of salted nuts and cocktails in the pen, but I thought I could detect a familiar tenderness in that area.

At last, I found a small furnished room above a bakery, and rented it. There I spent most of my time just lying on my bed, staring at the ceiling, a foot or two lower than could possibly have been legal, I was certain, in any known building code. I would receive support from the state for a little while, and actually had managed to set aside a sizeable amount of the profits from the prison typewriter business, so I didn't feel pressed to find a job. But for the first time in my life I was unable to move much farther than the convenience store down the street (and yes, it had been one of the victims in my "crime spree," but now bygones were bygones, and a different clerk than the one I had robbed — I don't know how this came up — actually had me pose for a picture wearing a bag and standing by the feet-and-inches scale by the front door).

Then one day — about 3:15 on a sunny afternoon — there I was, lying in bed when I suddenly remembered a story Emily told me, and it was one, strangely enough, that I had forgotten until that very moment. As best as I could remember, we were sitting on top of the cover for the pool pump, and Emily had been patting her clothes for a cigarette.

"This has been a pretty strange day," Emily had said. "It reminds me of a time I tried to visit the grave of a friend of mine, just an acquaintance, really, and I don't even know why I was going. He was someone I'd met at a party, and he died the very next day, but though we'd only talked for about twenty minutes, I still felt I had a connection. I was one of the last people to see him alive, after all, and so I owed it to him, I thought, to go out and see his grave and wish him good-bye. But I kept putting it off, you know. I'd be on the verge of leaving the house, and all at once would think of all the other things I needed to take care of, and the day would be over. Are you following me?"

I had nodded, I'm sure, though I have a feeling I wasn't paying as much attention at that point as I should have.

Emily continued, "So I started feeling worse and worse, until one day I just decided to put an end to it. I cleared my calendar, and packed a lunch, and went to bed with nothing scheduled for the next day but the visit. The next day was a Saturday, and it was a perfectly normal day, a little grayish, not particularly cold or windy, but by the time I finally got out of the house, and into the car, I had an urge for a cigarette. I'd never smoked in my life, but I drove to a convenience store that was on the way and bought a pack, and then I sat in the car and smoked one after another of those cigarettes, going through them like a prairie fire, wheezing, coughing, hacking, until I finally finished the whole bunch. Have you ever done anything like that?"

"No," I said, "I haven't."

Emily resumed. "I felt sick to my stomach, and was about to throw up. 'Well,' I said to myself, 'that's that. I guess that's going to be my smoking experience,' and I headed off toward the cemetery.

"But then while I was driving to the cemetery I started to think, how can anyone say they've had a smoking experience when they only smoked one pack? So even though I was sick to my stomach and the tips of my fingers were numb, I turned the car around and drove right back to the same store where I'd gotten the first pack. The second time I bought a menthol brand, and I finished that second pack in the parking lot, and was about to leave when I remembered I also had seen a low tar variety there that had looked interesting, so I went back in and bought it and smoked that too, without leaving the parking area. Then I threw up into a trash receptacle and fell asleep right there in the car, but it was too late. I was hooked, and I never did get to that grave. Eventually I even forgot his name, though I suppose I could have found that out easily enough.

"But sometimes," she said, "it feels like everything else in my whole life that's come afterward has just been a punishment for my failing to do that one simple, human thing."

And then she turned and kissed me.

Suddenly I realized that for the first time in years I was

lonely. I went downstairs to the bakery where I bought a loaf of fresh bread. Then I made a supper of cabbage and cheese to go with it. I washed the dishes and decided that the very next day I would go to the pet shop that was above where the Calypso used to be and buy myself a pet for company, something that wouldn't be too much trouble, a fish, perhaps, or a canary.

VI

That next day I woke up early — far too early as a matter of fact, because when I looked out my window I could see that the streetlights were still on and the street was completely empty. With nothing in particular to do, I stood there, wearing only a T-shirt I had found at the Treasure Chest, and my prison-issue shorts, wondering what name I should give my new pet. The shorts were surprisingly comfortable, and I hated to throw them away just because they had come from prison. Besides, they were the only real souvenir I had of doing "hard time," except for the personalized set of license plates the guys down in the shop had pressed for me: jet black letters that spelled out 1-TYPO-1 on a crisp white background. I could hardly wait to learn to drive so one day I could use them. An old Buick putt-putted by, turned the corner and disappeared. I thought about how much my life would change once I had a pet, and turned away from the window.

I flipped on the coffee machine (I'd remembered to set it up the night before) and looked for a piece of bread. Good luck!

— a whole slice plus a heel — so I put them both in the toaster. Then I pulled on a robe, socks, and used the bathroom, making a mental note to clean the toilet one of these days. I cut a melon; it dripped. The toast came up, burnt. I poured a cup of coffee; it spilled, and then I sat there, rereading yesterday's paper.

I walked back to the bathroom. As the shower filled with steam, I stood and admired the beach towel I'd picked up at the Treasure Chest. It showed an ocean scene with high waves breaking on stern rocks, and in the background an old-fashioned sailing ship about to go down. I'd gotten it for a quarter and I liked the sense of finality it produced. After the water got hot, I found the soap and lathered. I ran my hands up and down and all around my body to see if I could detect any changes; I couldn't, but who could tell? It might not be a bad idea to resume some of those exercises Dr. Pearlman had given me long ago, I decided. Then I rinsed, dressed, and had another cup of coffee. It was time to pick out my new companion.

The day was turning out to be fine, so instead of taking the bus, I decided to walk. Everything still had that oddish, what-is-wrong-with-this-picture quality to it that the passage of time can bring. Things were the same, yet, not exactly. I passed cleaners, thrift shops, other bakeries . . . and then there it was again, the old Calypso. The computer center that had occupied the site only days earlier had gone out of business, and a cardboard sign in the window announced a coffee shop would be opening soon. Still above it however, evidently solvent and looking just the way it had during my days with Sally (though it had been usually closed by the time I arrived at the Calypso), was The World of Animals.

I pushed the door open, and from somewhere above me a bell went off, followed by a virtual Bremen-town symphony orchestra of whines, scratches, rubs, chirps, barks, moans, squawks, and splashes. This was the first time I'd ever been inside, and I could see someone — a woman — working at the back of the shop.

"Don't worry," I shouted. "I'll just look around."

I bent down to study the pink-nosed, eager, mindless mice, and next to them the larger but equally mindless hamsters and guinea pigs. They had nothing to offer me in the way of real friendship though, and I felt a momentary stab of longing for Dominique, wherever she might be. I stood back up, feeling dizzy for a moment. I wondered if it was the two big cups of coffee I'd drunk at breakfast, or something more ominous, health-wise.

To clear my head, I walked over to the display of leashes. There were long ones, and short ones, and ones which, if you pushed a button, would send the poor mutt on the other end zinging back to where it started. There were leashes of metal, nylon, leather, and plastic, and on the wall behind them was a certificate of inspection by the Humane Society, made out to The World of Animals and its proprietor, Emily something-or-other (the last name had been abraded by what must have been years of leashes rubbing against it).

Could it be?

I whirled around, dizzy all over again. Holding on to the shelves for balance, I made my way slowly to the rear of the shop, where the woman I'd called out to was poking around in the fish tanks. Her hair, though longer and now with a touch of gray, was *her* hair, her skin *her* skin, the freckles across her shoulders very similar to the freckles I remembered from so long ago, and still, she hadn't turned around.

"Emily," I said.

Maybe I didn't say it loudly enough, or maybe the extremely annoying hum from the electric motors attached to the fish tanks to keep the water circulating made it so she couldn't hear me. She scooped a small, square net into the tank and expertly flipped out a dead guppy into a plastic cup that she was holding.

I took a deep breath. The shop hadn't yet been cleaned from overnight, an ammonia smell seared my lungs. "Emily," I said, "it's Paul."

She faced me, looking confused, and really I can't say that I blamed her.

"Emily," I said, "the pool," but the expression on her face remained blank.

I was embarrassed that I had to say it, but I did: "Organs, Emily. Human organs."

This time I could see that my words had struck home. She lay the net down and stared at me really hard. "You weren't by any chance," she said at last, "one of those poor people who bought their organ from that joint, were you? If so, I didn't have anything to do with it. I was only an employee, and for a very short time at that. For a while, it seemed they had every young girl in St. Nils babysitting that damn pool, so I'd say you're lucky to be alive, and if you're looking for someone to sue, you should try those doctors, not me."

"Emily," I said, "don't worry. I never got that organ. I'm not suing, but remember Paul? Remember that you once wrote a letter to a guy named Paul? Well, that Paul was me. I'm that

Paul, but I never got your letter until seven years later because the day before it arrived, I left for a free trip to Iceland with a rug cleaner. It may or may not have been a mistake, but you should know that in my heart I always intended to return."

Emily was beginning to gulp in an unusual fashion, so I continued: "Then a lot of other things happened that I can't get into at this moment, but here I am. I'm back, and though it's been twenty-one years since I've last seen you, I must say that except for a few gray hairs and the few tiny, and incidentally very attractive, wrinkles around your mouth and eyes, you seem not to have changed a bit. Your arms are as firm as ever, your breasts as high and round, your back is as straight, and your lips seem as luscious. Not that I care only about the physical, Emily, far from it — but both of us know that the spiritual and emotional aspects of a relationship take, and deserve, far more time, so I thought I'd better start with what's in front of me."

Emily took a deep breath. She had gotten her hiccups, or whatever they were, under control. "You should realize," she said, "that at one time in my life I wrote a lot of letters. It was a rough patch, if you know what I mean, and back then I think I must have been on some kind of drugs or something — I don't mean drugs, I mean medication. About half of those letters I was able to get back from the Post Office, usually the next morning before they were actually mailed, but unfortunately a lot of them went out anyway. I admit it was a big deal back then, but now it just seems like one of those things we all do when we're kids."

I could see that Emily's excitement over finding out what had happened to her letter had miraculously rinsed away the years, and I allowed myself to be diverted for a moment in appreciation of the mind's subtle mechanisms. There we both were, still in the aftershock of a powerful experience we had shared over twenty years ago, but my more focused, masculine mind had not released it, while hers, feminine, and more capable of enfolding multiple agendas, had simply let it float aimlessly around without necessarily feeling the need for some more permanent resolution as she went on with the rest of her life. Except for a two-inch scar over her left eyebrow, she looked just as I'd remembered her.

"Emily," I said, "That scar, I know you're probably self-conscious about it and everything, but I think it's beautiful."

"Thanks for your good thoughts," she said.

Then I couldn't hold it back any longer. "Emily," I said, "I'm dying."

"You're what?" she said, and she seemed to be having some difficulty confronting the powerful emotions that must have been resurfacing.

"Dying," I repeated. For a second, I thought that if only her scar had been half an inch higher, it would have looked a whole lot better.

"But I thought you said that you had gotten a transplant from somewhere else."

"I didn't," I said, but then when I tried to tell her about the salted nuts diet and its powers to arrest, if not actually cure, certain rare cases of orgagenic disintegration, she changed the subject back again.

"Dying . . . did you say you were dying?"

"Well," I said, "I could be."

"Listen," she said. "In that case, I have a kind of surprise for you. If you're willing to hang around the shop and make yourself useful till closing time, I think I have a thing you may find interesting."

To have found her after all these years — even if she had managed to repress large parts of our relationship — could she guess how important this day was to me? From time to time I would steal a peek at her to be sure it wasn't a dream, but there she remained, leaning on the counter next to the cash register, while I cleaned the pen of the pair of lop-eared rabbits, filled up the seed dish for the parrot, receiving a nasty bite in the process, and laid a dead canary to rest in the trash. Then I swept the floor and changed the sticks on the deodorizers. It was good to be working again.

At lunchtime I walked down to the local health-food store to pick up some wheat bread and cottage cheese for Emily (I might have known she was a vegetarian), and brought back a head of cabbage for myself. As we spread the food out on the counter, I could feel my eyes fill with tears. There I was, back with Emily, eating cabbage after all that time.

"What do I owe you?" Emily wanted to know.

"No charge," I said.

After lunch I picked up the broom and went over the floor again. Customers came and went. A shaven-headed, nose-pierced boy bought one of the mice to feed his entirely predictable snake, and a couple of little kids picked out a hamster. A gray-haired woman, after a lot of questions, wound up with a finch and took home an expensive cage.

Two men, Sheldon and Darnell, apparently regulars, came by to ask about a pet-sitter who could check on their cat while they went off on a ski trip to New Zealand, which they'd won as a result of pledging their support to their local Public

Radio station. "But all our excitement over our trip evaporated the moment we realized we would have to leave Shirley," Sheldon said, "because she's a very special kitty."

Emily looked through her files to search for the phone numbers of people who might be able to help, while I told the pair about Dominique and the unique relationship we had enjoyed. Sheldon and Darnell both seemed quite interested.

"Try these names," Emily finally offered, "and if they don't work, then call me back. I'll see what I can do." The grateful pair spent ninety-three dollars on cat toys and litter, and left.

Sheldon and Darnell were followed by an old man who bought five pounds of maggots. By day's end, I calculated Emily had sold almost a thousand dollars worth of merchandise, and things quieted down long enough for her to take up knitting a green sweater she said she'd been working on for a while. It was the exact shade of green as my favorite afghan, which had gotten lost in the shuffle of all those past years.

At last Emily locked the shop, and led me down the stairs to the alley where she had parked her car, a rusting, classic Mustang. The day was still warm, and the sun was high in the sky. "Put your seatbelt on," she told me.

She flipped to a jazz station on the radio, and the scenery shot by as in a movie. I rubbed my arms and my legs, which were becoming numb. I wondered if it was that organ business, or maybe just the Mustang's springs which were poking through the stained fabric of the front seat. It wasn't important. I sat back and let the late afternoon breeze, whistling in through the broken window on my side, drift over me. Emily could teach me to drive her car, I thought. Somehow, what with one thing and another, both in St. Nils and Iceland, I never exactly had a chance to learn, but now I could imagine Emily's small hand on mine, guiding me through the gears, the gentle pressure of her palm on my thigh to indicate when to push in the clutch, and her delicate fingers prompting my own through each motion of the turn signal. One day perhaps in the near future, my own license plate would be mounted on the back of this very car.

I shut my eyelids and breathed in the smell of Emily mixed with the smells of the countryside and a few squashed French fries on the car's hopelessly shredded carpet. Suddenly I remembered a story she had told me long ago, back at the pool. She had just jumped into the water following one of our acts of lovemaking ("The organs are getting anxious," she'd said. "This will just take a minute"), and meanwhile I was running back and forth along the pool's slippery deck to calm myself, when in the process I jammed the big toe of my left foot into one of the drain openings. I got it out easily enough, and Emily came up just in time to see me hopping around, holding my injured toe. It was then she said simply, "Pain . . . I could tell you a thing or two about that some day, if you were interested."

"I'm interested right now," I answered, and sat down on the deck, holding the affected toe above my head to slow the bleeding.

"Well," she said, "back in the days while I was growing up on the farm — I think I mentioned that earlier — it was my job, really the only job I actually had, to weed the fennel."

I must have given her a look, because she said, "That's right, you heard me: fennel. For some reason Lonnie and Brad had thought fennel was going to be the next big vegetable craze, and when it was, they used to say, they'd be rich. Of course, it turned out to be arugula.

"Anyway, there I was, weeding the fennel garden, and a light rain was starting to fall, a warm one, so that mixed with the fragrance of fresh fennel and the smells of the earth, the whole experience was actually very pleasant. And there I was, bent over, completely wet of course, wearing only a thin cotton dress and no underwear, my hands and knees brown with the mud, digging up the weeds with a screwdriver, and not even one of those proper weeding tools that has a wooden handle and a flat blade with a little notch at the end for prying out extra tough stems, because Brad was too cheap to get one of those things, when, maybe because it was wet and so slippery, I was working away on a particularly difficult weed, and the screwdriver somehow slipped upwards and stuck itself smack in the middle of my forearm, where it just stayed. It felt as though I'd been hit by lightning so I shut my eyes and everything went white, then orange, then purple, and finally black, which was when I lost consciousness for a while. Let me tell you," she concluded, "that really hurt."

Now decades later, I was keeping my own eyes shut. I could picture the young girl in the story, muddy and passed out cold in the fennel field, and then the woman who had told me this story, naked and dripping at the edge of the pool, and finally the mature but still lovely person sitting beside me right now, the three of them, like the three circles of a special 3-D gun sight, lined up to form a single glowing ring. I could smell the fennel, and the salt from the solution that had bathed the organs, and Emily's perfume.

The Mustang hit a bump, and I opened my eyes. Emily

was still there, right next to me. I was happy, of course, but surprisingly also found myself slightly ashamed to notice how completely all my earlier thoughts about obtaining an animal companion had vanished.

We drove up some hills and down some others. We passed several fields of grain ready for the harvest, and the ripples caused by the wind gave me the impression that the wheat, or whatever it was, was actually running alongside her car. Mile after mile we traveled. Emily told me how it seemed to her that the ripe wheat was like a blank page waiting to be filled by someone's story, and I was just about to tell her how a long time ago I'd had much the same thought, when all at once the Mustang's engine died. We glided to a stop at the side of the road, and I looked at Emily.

"What happened?" I said.

"I don't know," she told me.

Emily tried the ignition, and though the car's engine wheezed and coughed, nothing happened.

"Does that gas gauge work?" I asked her. "Because if it does, we're in trouble."

I gave it a tap and the needle just lay there. Unfortunately, Emily said, it just happened to be the sole functioning instrument on the Mustang's smeared and pitted instrument panel.

She shut off the radio, and the place — except for the twittering birds, the buzzing insects, and the wind — was eerily silent. I stared at her and she stared back, as if there was something she was about to say but couldn't quite bring herself to. We opened the trunk and looked inside for a can of gas; save for a dust-covered ice chest, the trunk was empty. "Well," I said, and she shrugged.

Then in the distance I saw a car approaching. I stepped out onto the road and began to wave. Eventually a dark blue Volvo pulled up in front of the Mustang. On the right side of its back bumper was a sticker that read "Immortality," with an arrow pointing to the right. On its left was one for animal rights. Then the car's doors opened with a squeak, and who should get out but Sheldon and Darnell.

"I think we're out of gas, " I said.

"Where were you headed?" Sheldon asked.

"I don't actually know," I answered.

"Cliff View," Emily said, and they nodded like they knew exactly what she was talking about, but as long as I'd lived in St. Nils, I'd never heard of it, or if I had, I'd forgotten.

"We heard of a really nice boarding hotel for cats called Kitty Villa. We're going there now to check it out. We can drop you off, pick up a can of gas, and then pick you up again on our way back," Sheldon said.

"Well now," Emily told them, "If you had only asked earlier I could have told you that Kitty Villa has an excellent reputation, though it may be a bit on the pricey side."

The sun was sliding toward the horizon, but hadn't yet quite touched it when we arrived at our (even if I hadn't been exactly sure where we were going) destination. Cliff View turned out to be the oldest cemetery in the area, with just a few dozen graves looking over the ocean, and was surrounded by a low wall of crumbling stone.

"This is just about my favorite spot in the world," Emily said.

Sheldon stopped and let us out.

"We'll be back in about an hour," Darnell said. "Don't worry."

They drove off and we walked in silence along the bluff that overlooked the ocean, the surface of which flared up in the setting sun to greet the two of us like some old memory. But Emily's, or mine? That was the question. The sea was calm that day, and except where the waves were breaking, it was as smooth as the nap of an endless rug.

Emily took my hand in her smaller one. "I wanted you to see this," she said.

I wondered what she could possibly have in mind.

I followed her down the aisles of monuments. The cemetery was an old-fashioned one, with the ground collapsed above some of the graves, while around others, possibly because of the superior quality of their coffins, the ground had dropped, leaving mounds like low, modern coffee tables. Here and there were dry and stunted pine trees. Doves walked around where the trees had pushed out of the dry ground and cheerlessly pecked at invisible seeds, flaring their feathers into the air from time to time at imagined danger.

There were marble and slate slabs marking all those dead who were buried beneath them, making me think, despite myself, of the trash can containing all those potential pets back at The World of Animals, those mice and fish and birds, with their own proud strutting, their own pointless revolutions of the exercise wheel, their own foggy memories, their chirps, their squeals of joy and pain. And what was so different really, between this quiet spot and the can in Emily's store?

We almost stepped on a collection of tools lying beneath a bush — a couple of shovels, a pick, and a rake.

"It looks like the gravediggers left them," Emily said.

"It looks as if nobody's touched them for weeks," I told her. They were dusty, and weeds seemed to have sprouted around them. I turned around slowly. I couldn't see any new graves, any fresh soil, not even any wilting pots of geraniums left by tenderhearted visitors. The place was deserted, all right. Beyond everything, the sea glowed as if beneath its sleeping surface there was a fire, a heap of coals waiting for a barbecue. Gulls called, hovering off the cliff's edge where the cemetery ended, and the grass there crumbled in helpless chunks down to the rocks and sea far below. The air was still warm, even though it was approaching evening.

"Wait," Emily said, and then she walked off for a minute, over toward the edge of the cliff. It seemed as if she had something on her mind. When she came back she took my hand once again, and led me in silence to a single limestone marker, with "Valerie" carved in plain black letters.

"A few years ago," she said, "I purchased the plot right next to this grave at a government auction. It was a sad story, really. They told me a man had bought both of those spots for himself and his wife, and then she died, and after that he traveled to a foreign land where he disappeared. They were selling his estate to pay his back taxes."

What was Emily trying to say? I looked at the space waiting there next to the simple grave; it was only dirt, but seemed vulnerable, and somehow friendly. I was confused. The wind started to rise, blowing warm air through Emily's hair. Far below, the waves exploded on their rocks in a loud and salty spray.

"I always imagined being buried here myself one day,"

Emily told me, "but now I'm not so sure. I've been reading books on cryonics, and to tell the truth, a part of me thinks that's the route I want to take. Except for the fact that I probably won't remember anything that happened while I was alive, it doesn't seem like such a bad thing."

She stopped to check my reaction, so I nodded.

"And now, Paul, you say you're dying, so I'll tell you what: I'll let you buy the gravesite for four hundred dollars."

I admit to being confused for a moment. Was I wrong to have expected our relationship to resume so quickly after all these years? Or was Emily's course the wiser: to begin on a more mundane level, that of a simple business transaction, and to gradually build up trust before wading out past the breakers of the heart over our heads.

I looked out at the ocean again, moving and unmoving as usual. "Give me a minute," I said, and walked to the other end of the cemetery, where the end of the horseshoe made by the cliff curved back out to the ocean. A hundred feet below, at the bottom of the cliff, the water rushed up to the rocks strewn with seaweed and tethered plants and then retreated slowly. I looked back at the rim of the bluff, where it swung toward the horseshoe's opposing side, where Emily was standing. Beneath her, though she couldn't see them, working their way out of the crumbling cliff, were the square, blind ends of ancient coffins, poking their heads into the air above the water like open-mouthed, hungry birds. Here and there, where the wood on the end of them had let go before the erosion of the cliff had a chance to loosen the entire box, were the bones of arms and legs, and gleaming caps of skulls, about to topple downward. This whole place was melting fast. Who could tell how long anything was going to last, I thought. A few good storms, a couple years, and that would be me or somebody else, falling into the water, never to be reconstituted, with or without memories. I walked back to where Emily was standing.

"What do you say?" she asked me. "You won't find many places prettier than this. I know this guy's wife is a stranger, but then you've got all eternity to get to know each other.

"Just joking," she added.

I stared out at the ocean. I was getting an idea. "Well," I finally said, "will you take three hundred for it?"

"Three-fifty," she said.

I fished inside my pocket and pulled out three hundred-dollar bills, a twenty, and three tens. "It's a deal."

Emily held the hundreds up to the light for a minute. They were real, of course. Then she kissed me on the cheek. "You're sweet," she said.

I hadn't been so happy in a long while, but remembered just in time Mitzie's advice would be to take it slow, so I strolled over to where the tools were lying, and picked up a shovel. This was now my property. I could do anything I liked with it. I carried the shovel over to the land I'd just acquired, and stuck its tip in the ground. It felt good. I pushed it down a little farther, then lifted out some dirt. It occurred to me that this was an old place. Who knew what might be buried there? I put the shovel in the dirt again and pulled it out. A disk of dark, corroded metal fell next to my feet. It was the top half of an empty ribbon spool of an old Underwood portable, from before they started making them out of plastic. I brushed it off, stuck it in my pocket, and dug down a little more.

By the time I looked up again Sheldon and Darnell's Volvo

had arrived at the cemetery's entrance, and I could tell by the blue smoke coming from the Mustang's exhaust that they had gotten it going.

The Volvo drove off.

"Hey!" I could hear Emily calling. "It's time to leave."

But it felt good to be digging there in the cool of dusk, with the noise of the ocean and the birds. The air was still for a minute, caught in that small pause that happens when the wind switches from blowing inland to back out to sea again.

I walked beneath one of the trees and sat down on a bench. The shade was everywhere by then, and the sun had dropped beneath the horizon.

"Paul," I could hear Emily shout. "What are you doing?"

I stared at the ground I'd just purchased. It was mine, I thought, as deep as I wanted to go.

A few birds chirped.

Waves crashed.

For a moment a bug got stuck in my hair, but then it found its way out.

When I looked up again it had gotten so dark that I couldn't be certain if the Mustang was there or not.

I remained right where I was. It was possible that Emily had walked over to get me, but it was too dark to tell that either.

"Emily," I said, "I see you."

END

I would like to thank Mary Otis, Janice Shapiro, Gary Walkow, Monona Wali, Isabel Fonseca, and Michael Silverblatt for their generous encouragement and suggestions, as well as the unwitting complicity of Friederike Mayröcker, whose book of poems, *with each clouded peak,* provided the inspiration for several sections of this writing.

ELECTED DALKEY ARCHIVE PAPERBACKS

FOR A FULL LIST OF PUBLICATIONS, VISIT:
www.dalkeyarchive.com

SELECTED DALKEY ARCHIVE PAPERBACK

FOR A FULL LIST OF PUBLICATIONS, VISIT
www.dalkeyarchive.com